Arthur Conan Doyle was a British author, physician and spiritualist who created the fictional detective Sherlock Holmes. Holmes featured in a number of novels and short stories, most of which have remained in print for well over a century. Arthur Conan Doyle's best-known works include the novels: *A Study in Scarlet*, *The Sign of the Four*, *The Stark Munro Letters* and *The Hound of the Baskervilles*; short-story collections: *The Adventures of Sherlock Holmes*, *Round the Red Lamp: Being Facts and Fancies of Medical Life* and *Danger! and Other Stories* and works of historical non-fiction: *The Crime of the Congo* and *The Great Boer War*.

D1571348

the **VERY BEST** of SHERLOCK HOLMES

Arthur Conan Doyle

▼▼▼▼

Introduction by RUSKIN BOND

talking
CUB

TALKING CUB
Published by Speaking Tiger Publishing Pvt. Ltd
4381/4 Ansari Road, Daryaganj,
New Delhi–110002, India

ISBN: 978-93-87164-40-6
eISBN: 978-93-87164-22-2

10 9 8 7 6 5 4 3 2 1

Typset in Adobe Garamond Pro by Jojy Philip
Printed at Sanat Printers, Kundli

contents

introduction

Growing up, some of my favourite books involved detectives who solved all kinds of devious crimes. I read so many of these stories that I became somewhat of an expert in figuring out the various types of crimes and how to guess the criminal. There were the murder mysteries, of course, at which writers like Agatha Christie excelled. Here there would be the locked-room mysteries, or stories where the murderer was known, yet one kept wondering how he or she did it, and then there were stories where you kept guessing till the last grand revelation.

The other great writer here was, of course, Arthur Conan Doyle with his Sherlock Holmes stories. With Holmes, Conan Doyle brought about a startling change in the way fictional detectives lived and worked. Holmes was a bit of an eccentric, and his methods of deduction would surprise his readers as much as they did the characters in the books. There he would sit, smoking his pipe, and just by noticing an ink stain on a finger or a bit of mud on the boots, he would be able to tell everything about where the person had been, what he or she had been doing, and many other details of his life. And when his faithful Watson would demand an explanation, it would all seem remarkably simple.

The stories of Sherlock Holmes are true classics in the manner in which they have survived and thrived over the many years since they first appeared in print. The books continue to be published and read by every new generation of readers. I am told that this is fuelled by the numerous movie and television adaptations of Sherlock Holmes. Somewhere in these stories there are elements that bright young scriptwriters of today can pick up and plug in to create newer versions. It's all elementary, one might say! Yet, the real joy still lies in reading the stories in their true original form, within the pages of a book.

To this end, in this collection I have brought together six of the very best Holmes stories. And why do I say these are the best? Well, for one, I have read them many times since my schooldays and enjoyed each one of these every time. But there is a further interesting twist to this selection. In 1927, *Strand* magazine of London had a competition, where they asked their readers to rank the best Sherlock Holmes stories. When the entries started coming in, who better to ask for his opinion about the very best stories than the writer himself? So Arthur Conan Doyle sat down and created a list of twelve of his favourite Sherlock adventures. These are not just favourites because of some obscure authorly reason. Doyle wrote a short piece that was published in the *Strand* that gave his reasons for picking these twelve. In this book, for reasons of space, we are carrying six of the twelve. The article by Doyle in which he mentions his reasons for choosing the twelve is also reproduced here.

It is, of course, well known that Doyle did not always share the same affection for Sherlock Holmes as his readers. He was also a remarkable writer of science fiction with works like *The Lost World* and of several works of historical fiction. These other works were possibly closer to his heart. Yet, it was thanks to Sherlock Holmes that he received world-wide acclaim. Tired of Holmes forever hijacking his writing life, Doyle even killed off Holmes with a fall down a cliff while battling his nemesis Professor Moriarty. This story, 'The Final Problem', appears in this book. However, the reading public had very strong opinions on this matter, and they would not let Doyle rest till he brought Holmes back from the dead. Happily for them, Holmes enjoyed a long and successful career following his fall, and appeared in stories that were published till 1927.

And so, here he is once again, and it is time to sit back and dip into the incredible adventures of Sherlock Holmes, Doctor John Watson, Professor Moriarty, and a host of other characters. From conspiracies to secret societies, deadly animals to deadlier poisons, these stories have them all. Be sure to keep your eyes open, and a light handy, for these stories stop for no one and no bedtime!

Ruskin Bond
Landour, Mussoorie

how i made my list

When this competition was first mooted I went into it in a most light-hearted way, thinking that it would be the easiest thing in the world to pick out the twelve best of the Holmes stories. In practice I found that I had engaged myself in a serious task. In the first place I had to read the stories myself with some care. 'Step, steep, weary work,' as the Scottish landlady remarked.

I began by eliminating altogether the last twelve stories, which are scattered through the *Strand* for the last five or six years. They are about to come out in a volume form under the title *The Casebook of Sherlock Holmes*, but the public could not easily get at them. Had they been available I should have put two of them in my team—namely, 'The Lion's Mane' and 'The Illustrious Client'. The first of these is hampered by being told by Holmes himself, a method which I employed only twice, as it certainly cramps the narrative. On the other hand, the actual plot is among the very best of the whole series, and for that it deserves its place. 'The Illustrious Client', on the other hand, is not remarkable for plot, but it has a certain dramatic quality and moves adequately in lofty circles, so I should also have found a place for it.

However, these being ruled out, I am now faced with some forty odd candidates to be weighed against each other. There are certainly some few an echo of which has come to me from all parts of the world, and I think this is the final proof of merit of some sort. There is the grim story 'The Speckled Band'. That I am sure will be on every list. Next to that in popular favour and in my own esteem I would place 'The Red-Headed League' and 'The Dancing Men', on account in each case of the originality of the plot. Then we could hardly leave out the story which deals with the only foe who ever really extended Holmes, and which deceived the public (and Watson) into the erroneous inference of his death. Also, I think the first story of all should go in, as it opened the path for the others, and it has more female interest than is usual. Finally, I think the story which essays the difficult task of explaining away the alleged death of Holmes, and which also introduces such a villain as Colonel Sebastian Moran, should also have a place. This puts 'The Final Problem', 'A Scandal in Bohemia' and 'The Empty House' upon our list, and we have got our first half-dozen.

But now comes the crux. There are a number of stories which really are a little hard to separate. On the whole I think I should find a place for 'The Five Orange Pips', for though it is short it has a certain dramatic quality of its own. So now only five places are left. There are two stories which deal with high diplomacy and intrigue. They are both among the very best of the series. The one is 'The Naval Treaty' and the other 'The Second Stain'. There is no room for both of them in the team, and on the whole I regard the latter as the better story. Therefore we will put it down for the eighth place.

And now which? 'The Devil's Foot' has points. It is grim and new. We will give it the ninth place. I think also that 'The Priory School' is worth a place if only for the dramatic moment when Holmes points his finger at the Duke. I have only two places left. I hesitate between 'Silver Blaze', 'The Bruce-Partington Plans', 'The Crooked Man', 'The Man with the Twisted Lip', 'The Gloria Scott', 'The Greek Interpreter', 'The Reigate Squires', 'The Musgrave Ritual' and 'The Resident Patient'. On what principle am I to choose two out of those? The racing detail in 'Silver Blaze' is very faulty, so we must disqualify him. There is little to choose between the others. A small thing would turn the scale. 'The Musgrave Ritual' has a historical touch which gives it a little added distinction. It also has a memory from Holmes' early life. So now we come to the very last. I might as well draw the name out of a bag, for I see no reason to put one before the other. Whatever their merit—and I make no claim for that—they are all as good as I could make them. On the whole, Holmes himself shows perhaps the most ingenuity in 'The Reigate Squires', and therefore this shall be twelfth in my team.

It is proverbially a mistake for a judge to give his reasons, but I have analyzed mine if only to show any competitors that I really have taken some trouble in the matter.

A. Conan Doyle
Published in *Strand*, 1927

the adventure of the speckled band

On glancing over my notes of the seventy odd cases in which I have during the last eight years studied the methods of my friend Sherlock Holmes, I find many tragic, some comic, a large number merely strange, but none commonplace; for, working as he did rather for the love of his art than for the acquirement of wealth, he refused to associate himself with any investigation which did not tend towards the unusual, and even the fantastic. Of all these varied cases, however, I cannot recall any which presented more singular features than that which was associated with the well-known Surrey family of the Roylotts of Stoke Moran. The events in question occurred in the early days of my association with Holmes, when we were sharing rooms as bachelors in Baker Street. It is possible that I might have placed them upon record before, but a promise of secrecy was made at the time, from which I have only been freed during the last month by the untimely death of the lady to whom the pledge was given. It is perhaps as well that the facts should now come to light, for I have reasons to know that there are widespread rumours as to the death of Dr Grimesby Roylott which tend to make the matter even more terrible than the truth.

It was early in April in the year '83 that I woke one morning to find Sherlock Holmes standing, fully dressed, by the side of my bed. He was a late riser, as a rule, and as the clock on the mantelpiece showed me that it was only a quarter-past seven, I blinked up at him in some surprise, and perhaps just a little resentment, for I was myself regular in my habits.

'Very sorry to knock you up, Watson,' said he, 'but it's the common lot this morning. Mrs Hudson has been knocked up, she retorted upon me, and I on you.'

'What is it, then—a fire?'

'No; a client. It seems that a young lady has arrived in a considerable state of excitement, who insists upon seeing me. She is waiting now in the sitting-room. Now, when young ladies wander about the metropolis at this hour of the morning, and knock sleepy people up out of their beds, I presume that it is something very pressing which they have to communicate. Should it prove to be an interesting case, you would, I am sure, wish to follow it from the outset. I thought, at any rate, that I should call you and give you the chance.'

'My dear fellow, I would not miss it for anything.'

I had no keener pleasure than in following Holmes in

his professional investigations, and in admiring the rapid deductions, as swift as intuitions, and yet always founded on a logical basis with which he unravelled the problems which were submitted to him. I rapidly threw on my clothes and was ready in a few minutes to accompany my friend down to the sitting-room. A lady dressed in black and heavily veiled, who had been sitting in the window, rose as we entered.

'Good-morning, madam,' said Holmes cheerily. 'My name is Sherlock Holmes. This is my intimate friend and associate, Dr Watson, before whom you can speak as freely as before myself. Ha! I am glad to see that Mrs Hudson has had the good sense to light the fire. Pray draw up to it, and I shall order you a cup of hot coffee, for I observe that you are shivering.'

'It is not cold which makes me shiver,' said the woman in a low voice, changing her seat as requested.

'What then?'

'It is fear, Mr Holmes. It is terror.' She raised her veil as she spoke, and we could see that she was indeed in a pitiable state of agitation, her face all drawn and grey, with restless frightened eyes, like those of some hunted animal. Her features and figure were those of a woman of thirty, but her hair was shot with premature grey, and her expression was weary and haggard. Sherlock Holmes ran her over with one of his quick, all-comprehensive glances.

'You must not fear,' said he soothingly, bending forward and patting her forearm. 'We shall soon set matters right,

I have no doubt. You have come in by train this morning, I see.'

'You know me, then?'

'No, but I observe the second half of a return ticket in the palm of your left glove. You must have started early, and yet you had a good drive in a dog-cart, along heavy roads, before you reached the station.'

The lady gave a violent start and stared in bewilderment at my companion.

'There is no mystery, my dear madam,' said he, smiling. 'The left arm of your jacket is spattered with mud in no less than seven places. The marks are perfectly fresh. There is no vehicle save a dog-cart which throws up mud in that way, and then only when you sit on the left-hand side of the driver.'

'Whatever your reasons may be, you are perfectly correct,' said she. 'I started from home before six, reached Leatherhead at twenty past, and came in by the first train to Waterloo. Sir, I can stand this strain no longer; I shall go mad if it continues. I have no one to turn to—none, save only one, who cares for me, and he, poor fellow, can be of little aid. I have heard of you, Mr Holmes; I have heard of you from Mrs Farintosh, whom you helped in the hour of her sore need. It was from her that I had your address. Oh, sir, do you not think that you could help me, too, and at least throw a little light through the dense darkness which surrounds me? At present it is out of my power to reward you for your services, but in a month or six weeks I shall be married, with the control of my own income, and then at least you shall not find me ungrateful.'

Holmes turned to his desk and, unlocking it, drew out a small case-book, which he consulted.

'Farintosh,' said he. 'Ah yes, I recall the case; it was concerned with an opal tiara. I think it was before your time, Watson. I can only say, madam, that I shall be happy to devote the same care to your case as I did to that of your friend. As to reward, my profession is its own reward; but you are at liberty to defray whatever expenses I may be put to, at the time which suits you best. And now I beg that you will lay before us everything that may help us in forming an opinion upon the matter.'

'Alas!' replied our visitor, 'the very horror of my situation lies in the fact that my fears are so vague, and my suspicions depend so entirely upon small points, which might seem trivial to another, that even he to whom of all others I have a right to look for help and advice looks upon all that I tell him about it as the fancies of a nervous woman. He does not say so, but I can read it from his soothing answers and averted eyes. But I have heard, Mr Holmes, that you can see deeply into the manifold wickedness of the human heart. You may advise me how to walk amid the dangers which encompass me.'

'I am all attention, madam.'

'My name is Helen Stoner, and I am living with my stepfather, who is the last survivor of one of the oldest Saxon families in England, the Roylotts of Stoke Moran, on the western border of Surrey.'

Holmes nodded his head. 'The name is familiar to me,' said he.

'The family was at one time among the richest in England, and the estates extended over the borders into Berkshire in the north, and Hampshire in the west. In the last century, however, four successive heirs were of a dissolute and wasteful disposition, and the family ruin was eventually completed by a gambler in the days of the Regency. Nothing was left save a few acres of ground, and the two-hundred-year-old house, which is itself crushed under a heavy mortgage. The last squire dragged out his existence there, living the horrible life of an aristocratic pauper; but his only son, my stepfather, seeing that he must adapt himself to the new conditions, obtained an advance from a relative, which enabled him to take a medical degree and went out to Calcutta, where, by his professional skill and his force of character, he established a large practice. In a fit of anger, however, caused by some robberies which had been perpetrated in the house, he beat his native butler to death and narrowly escaped a capital sentence. As it was, he suffered a long term of imprisonment and afterwards returned to England a morose and disappointed man.

'When Dr Roylott was in India he married my mother, Mrs Stoner, the young widow of Major-General Stoner, of the Bengal Artillery. My sister Julia and I were twins, and we were only two years old at the time of my mother's re-marriage. She had a considerable sum of money—not less than 1,000 pounds a year—and this she bequeathed to Dr Roylott entirely while we resided with him, with a provision that a certain annual sum should be allowed to each of us in the event of our marriage. Shortly after our return to England my mother died—she was killed eight years ago in a railway accident near Crewe. Dr Roylott then abandoned his attempts to establish himself in practice in London and took us to live with him in the old ancestral house at Stoke Moran. The money which my mother had left was enough for all our wants, and there seemed to be no obstacle to our happiness.

'But a terrible change came over our stepfather about this time. Instead of making friends and exchanging visits with our neighbours, who had at first been overjoyed to see a Roylott of Stoke Moran back in the old family seat, he shut himself up in his house and seldom came out save to indulge in ferocious quarrels with whoever might cross his path. Violence of temper approaching to mania has been hereditary in the men of the family, and in my stepfather's case it had, I believe, been intensified by his long residence in the tropics. A series of disgraceful brawls took place, two of which ended in the police-court, until at last he became the terror of the village, and the folks would fly at his approach, for he is a man of immense strength, and absolutely uncontrollable in his anger.

'Last week he hurled the local blacksmith over a parapet into a stream, and it was only by paying over all the money which I could gather together that I was able to avert another public exposure. He had no friends at all save the wandering gipsies, and he would give these vagabonds leave to encamp upon the few acres of bramble-covered land which represent the family estate, and would accept in return the hospitality of their tents, wandering away with them sometimes for weeks on end. He has a passion also for Indian animals, which are sent over to him by a correspondent, and he has at this moment a cheetah and a baboon, which wander freely over his grounds and are feared by the villagers almost as much as their master.

'You can imagine from what I say that my poor sister Julia and I had no great pleasure in our lives. No servant would stay with us, and for a long time we did all the work of the house. She was but thirty at the time of her death, and yet her hair had already begun to whiten, even as mine has.'

'Your sister is dead, then?'

'She died just two years ago, and it is of her death that I wish to speak to you. You can understand that, living the life which I have described, we were little likely to see anyone of our own age and position. We had, however, an aunt, my mother's maiden sister, Miss Honoria Westphail, who lives near Harrow, and we were occasionally allowed to pay short visits at this lady's house. Julia went there at Christmas two years ago, and met there a half-pay major of marines, to whom she became engaged. My stepfather learned of the engagement when my sister returned and offered no objection to the marriage; but within a fortnight of the day which had been fixed for the wedding, the terrible event occurred which has deprived me of my only companion.'

Sherlock Holmes had been leaning back in his chair with his eyes closed and his head sunk in a cushion, but he half opened his lids now and glanced across at his visitor.

'Pray be precise as to details,' said he.

'It is easy for me to be so, for every event of that dreadful time is seared into my memory. The manor-house is, as I have already said, very old, and only one wing is now inhabited. The bedrooms in this wing are on the ground floor, the sitting-rooms being in the central block of the buildings. Of these bedrooms the first is Dr Roylott's, the second my sister's, and the third my own. There is no communication between them, but they all open out into the same corridor. Do I make myself plain?'

'Perfectly so.'

'The windows of the three rooms open out upon the lawn. That fatal night Dr Roylott had gone to his room early, though we knew that he had not retired to rest, for my sister was troubled by the smell of the strong Indian cigars which it was his custom to smoke. She left her room, therefore, and came into mine, where she sat for some time, chatting about her approaching wedding. At eleven o'clock she rose to leave me, but she paused at the door and looked back.

'"Tell me, Helen," said she, "have you ever heard anyone whistle in the dead of the night?"

'"Never," said I.

'"I suppose that you could not possibly whistle, yourself, in your sleep?"

'"Certainly not. But why?"

'"Because during the last few nights I have always, about three in the morning, heard a low, clear whistle. I am a light sleeper, and it has awakened me. I cannot tell where it came from—perhaps from the next room, perhaps from the lawn. I thought that I would just ask you whether you had heard it."

'"No, I have not. It must be those wretched gipsies in the plantation."

'"Very likely. And yet if it were on the lawn, I wonder that you did not hear it also."

'"Ah, but I sleep more heavily than you."

'"Well, it is of no great consequence, at any rate." She smiled back at me, closed my door, and a few moments later I heard her key turn in the lock.'

'Indeed,' said Holmes. 'Was it your custom always to lock yourselves in at night?'

'Always.'

'And why?'

'I think that I mentioned to you that the doctor kept a cheetah and a baboon. We had no feeling of security unless our doors were locked.'

'Quite so. Pray proceed with your statement.'

'I could not sleep that night. A vague feeling of impending misfortune impressed me. My sister and I, you will recollect, were twins, and you know how subtle are the links which bind two souls which are so closely allied. It was a wild night. The wind was howling outside, and the rain was beating and splashing against the windows. Suddenly, amid all the hubbub of the gale, there burst forth the wild scream of a terrified woman. I knew that it was my sister's voice. I sprang from my bed, wrapped a shawl round me, and rushed into the corridor. As I opened my door I seemed to hear a low whistle, such as my sister described, and a few moments later a clanging sound, as if a mass of metal had fallen. As I ran down the passage, my sister's door was unlocked, and revolved slowly upon its hinges. I stared at it horror-stricken, not knowing what was about to issue from it. By the light of the corridor-lamp I saw my sister appear at the opening, her face blanched with terror, her hands groping for help, her whole figure swaying to and fro like that of a drunkard. I ran to her and threw my arms round her, but at that moment her knees seemed to give way and she fell to the ground. She writhed as one who is in terrible pain, and her limbs were dreadfully convulsed. At first I thought that she had not recognized me, but as I bent over her she suddenly shrieked out in a voice which I shall never forget, "Oh, my God! Helen! It was the band! The speckled band!" There was something else which she would fain have said, and she stabbed with her finger into the air in the direction of the doctor's room, but a fresh convulsion seized her and choked her words. I rushed out, calling loudly for my stepfather, and I met him hastening from his room in his dressing-gown. When he reached my sister's side she was unconscious, and though he poured brandy down her throat and sent for medical aid from the village, all efforts were in vain, for she slowly sank and died without having recovered her consciousness. Such was the dreadful end of my beloved sister.'

'One moment,' said Holmes, 'are you sure about this whistle and metallic sound? Could you swear to it?'

'That was what the county coroner asked me at the inquiry. It is my strong impression that I heard it, and yet, among the crash of the gale and the creaking of an old house, I may possibly have been deceived.'

'Was your sister dressed?'

'No, she was in her night-dress. In her right hand was found the charred stump of a match, and in her left a match-box.'

'Showing that she had struck a light and looked about her when the alarm took place. That is important. And what conclusions did the coroner come to?'

'He investigated the case with great care, for Dr Roylott's conduct had long been notorious in the county, but he was unable to find any satisfactory cause of death. My evidence showed that the door had been fastened upon the inner side, and the windows were blocked by old-fashioned shutters with broad iron bars, which were secured every night. The walls were carefully sounded, and were shown to be quite solid all round, and the flooring was also thoroughly examined, with the same result. The chimney is wide, but is barred up by four large staples. It is certain, therefore, that my sister was quite alone when she met her end. Besides, there were no marks of any violence upon her.'

'How about poison?'

'The doctors examined her for it, but without success.'

'What do you think that this unfortunate lady died of, then?'

'It is my belief that she died of pure fear and nervous shock, though what it was that frightened her I cannot imagine.'

'Were there gipsies in the plantation at the time?'

'Yes, there are nearly always some there.'

'Ah, and what did you gather from this allusion to a band—a speckled band?'

'Sometimes I have thought that it was merely the wild talk of delirium, sometimes that it may have referred to some band of people, perhaps to these very gipsies in the plantation. I do not know whether the spotted handkerchiefs which so many of them wear over their heads might have suggested the strange adjective which she used.'

Holmes shook his head like a man who is far from being satisfied.

'These are very deep waters,' said he, 'pray go on with your narrative.'

'Two years have passed since then, and my life has been until lately lonelier than ever. A month ago, however, a dear friend, whom I have known for many years, has done me the honour to ask my hand in marriage. His name is Armitage—Percy Armitage—the second son of Mr Armitage, of Crane Water, near Reading. My stepfather has offered no opposition to the match, and we are to be married in the course of the spring. Two days ago some repairs were started in the west wing of the building, and my bedroom wall has been pierced, so that I have had to move into the chamber in which my sister died, and to sleep in the very bed in which she slept. Imagine, then, my thrill of terror when last night, as I lay awake, thinking over her terrible fate, I suddenly heard in the silence of the night the low whistle which had been the herald of her own death. I sprang up and lit the lamp, but nothing was to be seen in the room. I was too shaken to go to bed again, however, so I dressed, and as soon as it was daylight I slipped down, got a dog-cart at the Crown Inn, which is opposite, and drove to Leatherhead, from whence I have come on this morning with the one object of seeing you and asking your advice.'

'You have done wisely,' said my friend. 'But have you told me all?'

'Yes, all.'

'Miss Roylott, you have not. You are screening your stepfather.'

'Why, what do you mean?'

For answer Holmes pushed back the frill of black lace which fringed the hand that lay upon our visitor's knee. Five little livid spots, the marks of four fingers and a thumb, were printed upon the white wrist.

'You have been cruelly used,' said Holmes.

The lady coloured deeply and covered over her injured wrist. 'He is a hard man,' she said, 'and perhaps he hardly knows his own strength.'

There was a long silence, during which Holmes leaned his chin upon his hands and stared into the crackling fire.

'This is a very deep business,' he said at last. 'There are a thousand details which I should desire to know before I decide upon our course of action. Yet we have not a moment to lose. If we were to come to Stoke Moran to-day, would it be possible for us to see over these rooms without the knowledge of your stepfather?'

'As it happens, he spoke of coming into town to-day upon some most important business. It is probable that he will be away all day, and that there would be nothing to disturb you. We have a housekeeper now, but she is old and foolish, and I could easily get her out of the way.'

'Excellent. You are not averse to this trip, Watson?'

'By no means.'

'Then we shall both come. What are you going to do yourself?'

'I have one or two things which I would wish to do now that I am in town. But I shall return by the twelve o'clock train, so as to be there in time for your coming.'

'And you may expect us early in the afternoon. I have myself some small business matters to attend to. Will you not wait and breakfast?'

'No, I must go. My heart is lightened already since I have confided my trouble to you. I shall look forward to seeing you again this afternoon.' She dropped her thick black veil over her face and glided from the room.

'And what do you think of it all, Watson?' asked Sherlock Holmes, leaning back in his chair.

'It seems to me to be a most dark and sinister business.'

'Dark enough and sinister enough.'

'Yet if the lady is correct in saying that the flooring and walls are sound, and that the door, window, and chimney are impassable, then her sister must have been undoubtedly alone when she met her mysterious end.'

'What becomes, then, of these nocturnal whistles, and what of the very peculiar words of the dying woman?'

'I cannot think.'

'When you combine the ideas of whistles at night, the presence of a band of gipsies who are on intimate terms with this old doctor, the fact that we have every reason to believe that the doctor has an interest in preventing his stepdaughter's marriage, the dying allusion to a band, and, finally, the fact that Miss Helen Stoner heard a metallic clang, which might have been caused by one of those metal bars that secured the shutters falling back into its place, I think that there is good ground to think that the mystery may be cleared along those lines.'

'But what, then, did the gipsies do?'

'I cannot imagine.'

'I see many objections to any such theory.'

'And so do I. It is precisely for that reason that we are going to Stoke Moran this day. I want to see whether the objections are fatal, or if they may be explained away. But what in the name of the devil!'

The ejaculation had been drawn from my companion by the fact that our door had been suddenly dashed open, and that a huge man had framed himself in the aperture. His costume was a peculiar mixture of the professional and of the agricultural, having a black top-hat, a long frock-coat, and a pair of high gaiters, with a hunting-crop swinging in his hand. So tall was he that his hat actually brushed the cross bar of the doorway, and his breadth seemed to span it across from side to side. A large face, seared with a thousand wrinkles, burned yellow with the sun, and marked with every evil passion, was turned from one to the other of us, while his deep-set, bile-shot eyes, and his high, thin, fleshless nose, gave him somewhat the resemblance to a fierce old bird of prey.

'Which of you is Holmes?' asked this apparition.

'My name, sir; but you have the advantage of me,' said my companion quietly.

'I am Dr Grimesby Roylott, of Stoke Moran.'

'Indeed, Doctor,' said Holmes blandly. 'Pray take a seat.'

'I will do nothing of the kind. My stepdaughter has been here. I have traced her. What has she been saying to you?'

'It is a little cold for the time of the year,' said Holmes.

'What has she been saying to you?' screamed the old man furiously.

'But I have heard that the crocuses promise well,' continued my companion imperturbably.

'Ha! You put me off, do you?' said our new visitor, taking a step forward and shaking his hunting-crop. 'I know you, you scoundrel! I have heard of you before. You are Holmes, the meddler.'

My friend smiled.

'Holmes, the busybody!'

His smile broadened.

'Holmes, the Scotland Yard Jack-in-office!'

Holmes chuckled heartily. 'Your conversation is most entertaining,' said he. 'When you go out close the door, for there is a decided draught.'

'I will go when I have said my say. Don't you dare to meddle with my affairs. I know that Miss Stoner has been here. I traced her! I am a dangerous man to fall foul of! See here.' He stepped swiftly forward, seized the poker, and bent it into a curve with his huge brown hands.

'See that you keep yourself out of my grip,' he snarled, and hurling the twisted poker into the fireplace he strode out of the room.

'He seems a very amiable person,' said Holmes, laughing. 'I am not quite so bulky, but if he had remained I might have shown him that my grip was not much more feeble than his own.' As he spoke he picked up the steel poker and, with a sudden effort, straightened it out again.

'Fancy his having the insolence to confound me with the official detective force! This incident gives zest to our investigation, however, and I only trust that our little friend will not suffer from her imprudence in allowing this brute to trace her. And now, Watson, we shall order breakfast, and afterwards I shall walk down to Doctors' Commons, where I hope to get some data which may help us in this matter.'

It was nearly one o'clock when Sherlock Holmes

returned from his excursion. He held in his hand a sheet of blue paper, scrawled over with notes and figures.

'I have seen the will of the deceased wife,' said he. 'To determine its exact meaning I have been obliged to work out the present prices of the investments with which it is concerned. The total income, which at the time of the wife's death was little short of 1,100 pounds, is now, through the fall in agricultural prices, not more than 750 pounds. Each daughter can claim an income of 250 pounds, in case of marriage. It is evident, therefore, that if both girls had married, this beauty would have had a mere pittance, while even one of them would cripple him to a very serious extent. My morning's work has not been wasted, since it has proved that he has the very strongest motives for standing in the way of anything of the sort. And now, Watson, this is too serious for dawdling, especially as the old man is aware that we are interesting ourselves in his affairs; so if you are ready, we shall call a cab and drive to Waterloo. I should be very much obliged if you would slip your revolver into your pocket. An Eley's No. 2 is an excellent argument with gentlemen who can twist steel pokers into knots. That and a tooth-brush are, I think, all that we need.'

At Waterloo we were fortunate in catching a train for Leatherhead, where we hired a trap at the station inn and drove for four or five miles through the lovely Surrey lanes. It was a perfect day, with a bright sun and a few fleecy clouds in the heavens. The trees and wayside hedges were just throwing out their first green shoots, and the air was full of the pleasant smell of the moist earth. To me at least there was a strange contrast between the sweet promise of the spring and this sinister quest upon which we were engaged. My companion sat in the front of the trap, his arms folded, his hat pulled down over his eyes, and his chin sunk upon his breast, buried in the deepest thought. Suddenly, however, he started, tapped me on the shoulder, and pointed over the meadows.

'Look there!' said he.

A heavily timbered park stretched up in a gentle slope, thickening into a grove at the highest point. From amid the branches there jutted out the grey gables and high roof-tree of a very old mansion.

'Stoke Moran?' said he.

'Yes, sir, that be the house of Dr Grimesby Roylott,' remarked the driver.

'There is some building going on there,' said Holmes, 'that is where we are going.'

'There's the village,' said the driver, pointing to a cluster of roofs some distance to the left, 'but if you want to get to the house, you'll find it shorter to get over this stile, and so by the foot-path over the fields. There it is, where the lady is walking.'

'And the lady, I fancy, is Miss Stoner,' observed Holmes, shading his eyes. 'Yes, I think we had better do as you suggest.'

We got off, paid our fare, and the trap rattled back on its way to Leatherhead.

'I thought it as well,' said Holmes as we climbed the stile, 'that this fellow should think we had come here as architects, or on some definite business. It may stop his gossip. Good-afternoon, Miss Stoner. You see that we have been as good as our word.'

Our client of the morning had hurried forward to meet us with a face which spoke her joy. 'I have been waiting so eagerly for you,' she cried, shaking hands with us warmly. 'All has turned out splendidly. Dr Roylott has gone to town, and it is unlikely that he will be back before evening.'

'We have had the pleasure of making the doctor's acquaintance,' said Holmes, and in a few words he sketched out what had occurred. Miss Stoner turned white to the lips as she listened.

'Good heavens!' she cried, 'he has followed me, then.'

'So it appears.'

'He is so cunning that I never know when I am safe from him. What will he say when he returns?'

'He must guard himself, for he may find that there is someone more cunning than himself upon his track. You must lock yourself up from him to-night. If he is violent, we shall take you away to your aunt's at Harrow. Now, we must make the best use of our time, so kindly take us at once to the rooms which we are to examine.'

The building was of grey, lichen-blotched stone, with a high central portion and two curving wings, like the claws of a crab, thrown out on each side. In one of these wings the windows were broken and blocked with wooden boards, while the roof was partly caved in, a picture of ruin. The central portion was in little better repair, but the right-hand block was comparatively modern, and the blinds in the windows, with the blue smoke curling up from the chimneys, showed that this was where the family resided. Some scaffolding had been erected against the end wall, and the stone-work had been broken into, but there were no signs of any workmen at the moment of our visit. Holmes walked slowly up and down the ill-trimmed lawn and examined with deep attention the outsides of the windows.

'This, I take it, belongs to the room in which you used to sleep, the centre one to your sister's, and the one next to the main building to Dr Roylott's chamber?'

'Exactly so. But I am now sleeping in the middle one.'

'Pending the alterations, as I understand. By the way, there does not seem to be any very pressing need for repairs at that end wall.'

'There were none. I believe that it was an excuse to move me from my room.'

'Ah! that is suggestive. Now, on the other side of this narrow wing runs the corridor from which these three rooms open. There are windows in it, of course?'

'Yes, but very small ones. Too narrow for anyone to pass through.'

'As you both locked your doors at night, your rooms were unapproachable from that side. Now, would you have the kindness to go into your room and bar your shutters?'

Miss Stoner did so, and Holmes, after a careful examination through the open window, endeavoured in every way to force the shutter open, but without success. There was no slit through which a knife could be passed to raise the bar. Then with his lens he tested the hinges, but they were of solid iron, built firmly into the massive masonry. 'Hum!' said he, scratching his chin in some perplexity, 'my theory certainly presents some difficulties. No one could pass these shutters if they were bolted. Well, we shall see if the inside throws any light upon the matter.'

A small side door led into the whitewashed corridor from which the three bedrooms opened. Holmes refused to examine the third chamber, so we passed at once to the second, that in which Miss Stoner was now sleeping, and in which her sister had met with her fate. It was a homely little room, with a low ceiling and a gaping fireplace, after the fashion of old country-houses. A brown chest of drawers stood in one corner, a narrow white-counterpaned bed in another, and a dressing-table on the left-hand side of the window. These articles, with two small wicker-work chairs, made up all the furniture in the room save for a square of Wilton carpet in the centre. The boards round and the panelling of the walls were of brown, worm-eaten oak, so old and discoloured that it may have dated from the original building of the house. Holmes drew one of the chairs into a corner and sat silent, while his eyes travelled round and round and up and down, taking in every detail of the apartment.

'Where does that bell communicate with?' he asked at last pointing to a thick bell-rope which hung down beside the bed, the tassel actually lying upon the pillow.

'It goes to the housekeeper's room.'

'It looks newer than the other things?'

'Yes, it was only put there a couple of years ago.'

'Your sister asked for it, I suppose?'

'No, I never heard of her using it. We used always to get what we wanted for ourselves.'

'Indeed, it seemed unnecessary to put so nice a bell-pull there. You will excuse me for a few minutes while I satisfy myself as to this floor.' He threw himself down upon his face with his lens in his hand and crawled swiftly backward and forward, examining minutely the cracks between the boards. Then he did the same with the wood-work with which the chamber was panelled. Finally he walked over to the bed and spent some time in staring at it and in running his eye up and down the wall. Finally he took the bell-rope in his hand and gave it a brisk tug.

'Why, it's a dummy,' said he.

'Won't it ring?'

'No, it is not even attached to a wire. This is very interesting. You can see now that it is fastened to a hook just above where the little opening for the ventilator is.'

'How very absurd! I never noticed that before.'

'Very strange!' muttered Holmes, pulling at the rope. 'There are one or two very singular points about this room. For example, what a fool a builder must be to open a ventilator into another room, when, with the same trouble, he might have communicated with the outside air!'

'That is also quite modern,' said the lady.

'Done about the same time as the bell-rope?' remarked Holmes.

'Yes, there were several little changes carried out about that time.'

'They seem to have been of a most interesting character—dummy bell-ropes, and ventilators which do not ventilate. With your permission, Miss Stoner, we shall now carry our researches into the inner apartment.'

Dr Grimesby Roylott's chamber was larger than that of his stepdaughter, but was as plainly furnished. A camp-bed, a small wooden shelf full of books, mostly of a technical character, an armchair beside the bed, a plain wooden chair against the wall, a round table, and a large iron safe were the principal things which met the eye. Holmes walked slowly round and examined each and all of them with the keenest interest.

'What's in here?' he asked, tapping the safe.

'My stepfather's business papers.'

'Oh! you have seen inside, then?'

'Only once, some years ago. I remember that it was full of papers.'

'There isn't a cat in it, for example?'

'No. What a strange idea!'

'Well, look at this!' He took up a small saucer of milk which stood on the top of it.

'No; we don't keep a cat. But there is a cheetah and a baboon.'

'Ah, yes, of course! Well, a cheetah is just a big cat, and yet a saucer of milk does not go very far in satisfying its wants, I dare say. There is one point which I should wish to determine.' He squatted down in front of the wooden chair and examined the seat of it with the greatest attention.

'Thank you. That is quite settled,' said he, rising and putting his lens in his pocket. 'Hullo! Here is something intcresting!'

The object which had caught his eye was a small dog lash hung on one corner of the bed. The lash, however, was curled upon itself and tied so as to make a loop of whipcord.

'What do you make of that, Watson?'

'It's a common enough lash. But I don't know why it should be tied.'

'That is not quite so common, is it? Ah, me! it's a wicked world, and when a clever man turns his brains to crime it is the worst of all. I think that I have seen enough now, Miss Stoner, and with your permission we shall walk out upon the lawn.'

I had never seen my friend's face so grim or his brow so dark as it was when we turned from the scene of this investigation. We had walked several times up and down the lawn, neither Miss Stoner nor myself liking to break in upon his thoughts before he roused himself from his reverie.

'It is very essential, Miss Stoner,' said he, 'that you should absolutely follow my advice in every respect.'

'I shall most certainly do so.'

'The matter is too serious for any hesitation. Your life may depend upon your compliance.'

'I assure you that I am in your hands.'

'In the first place, both my friend and I must spend the night in your room.'

Both Miss Stoner and I gazed at him in astonishment.

'Yes, it must be so. Let me explain. I believe that that is the village inn over there?'

'Yes, that is the Crown.'

'Very good. Your windows would be visible from there?'

'Certainly.'

'You must confine yourself to your room, on pretence of a headache, when your stepfather comes back. Then when you hear him retire for the night, you must open the shutters of your window, undo the hasp, put your lamp there as a signal to us, and then withdraw quietly with everything which you are likely to want into the room which you used to occupy. I have no doubt that, in spite of the repairs, you could manage there for one night.'

'Oh, yes, easily.'

'The rest you will leave in our hands.'

'But what will you do?'

'We shall spend the night in your room, and we shall investigate the cause of this noise which has disturbed you.'

'I believe, Mr Holmes, that you have already made up your mind,' said Miss Stoner, laying her hand upon my companion's sleeve.

'Perhaps I have.'

'Then, for pity's sake, tell me what was the cause of my sister's death.'

'I should prefer to have clearer proofs before I speak.'

'You can at least tell me whether my own thought is correct, and if she died from some sudden fright.'

'No, I do not think so. I think that there was probably some more tangible cause. And now, Miss Stoner, we must leave you for if Dr Roylott returned and saw us our journey would be in vain. Good-bye, and be brave, for if you will do what I have told you, you may rest assured that we shall soon drive away the dangers that threaten you.'

Sherlock Holmes and I had no difficulty in engaging a bedroom and sitting-room at the Crown Inn. They were on the upper floor, and from our window we could command a view of the avenue gate, and of the inhabited wing of Stoke Moran Manor House. At dusk we saw Dr Grimesby Roylott drive past, his huge form looming up beside the little figure of the lad who drove him. The boy had some slight difficulty in undoing the heavy iron gates, and we heard the hoarse roar of the doctor's voice and saw the fury with which he shook his clinched fists at him. The trap drove on, and a few minutes later we saw a sudden light spring up among the trees as the lamp was lit in one of the sitting-rooms.

'Do you know, Watson,' said Holmes as we sat together in the gathering darkness, 'I have really some scruples as to taking you to-night. There is a distinct element of danger.'

'Can I be of assistance?'

'Your presence might be invaluable.'

'Then I shall certainly come.'

'It is very kind of you.'

'You speak of danger. You have evidently seen more in these rooms than was visible to me.'

'No, but I fancy that I may have deduced a little more. I imagine that you saw all that I did.'

'I saw nothing remarkable save the bell-rope, and what purpose that could answer I confess is more than I can imagine.'

'You saw the ventilator, too?'

'Yes, but I do not think that it is such a very unusual thing to have a small opening between two rooms. It was so small that a rat could hardly pass through.'

'I knew that we should find a ventilator before ever we came to Stoke Moran.'

'My dear Holmes!'

'Oh, yes, I did. You remember in her statement she said that her sister could smell Dr Roylott's cigar. Now, of course that suggested at once that there must be a communication between the two rooms. It could only be a small one, or it would have been remarked upon at the coroner's inquiry. I deduced a ventilator.'

'But what harm can there be in that?'

'Well, there is at least a curious coincidence of dates. A ventilator is made, a cord is hung, and a lady who sleeps in the bed dies. Does not that strike you?'

'I cannot as yet see any connection.'

'Did you observe anything very peculiar about that bed?'

'No.'

'It was clamped to the floor. Did you ever see a bed fastened like that before?'

'I cannot say that I have.'

'The lady could not move her bed. It must always be in the same relative position to the ventilator and to the rope—or so we may call it, since it was clearly never meant for a bell-pull.'

'Holmes,' I cried, 'I seem to see dimly what you are hinting at. We are only just in time to prevent some subtle and horrible crime.'

'Subtle enough and horrible enough. When a doctor does go wrong he is the first of criminals. He has nerve and he has knowledge. Palmer and Pritchard were among the heads of their profession. This man strikes even deeper, but I think, Watson, that we shall be able to strike deeper still. But we shall have horrors enough before the night is over; for goodness' sake let us have a quiet pipe and turn our minds for a few hours to something more cheerful.'

About nine o'clock the light among the trees was extinguished, and all was dark in the direction of the Manor House. Two hours passed slowly away, and then, suddenly, just at the stroke of eleven, a single bright light shone out right in front of us.

'That is our signal,' said Holmes, springing to his feet; 'it comes from the middle window.'

As we passed out he exchanged a few words with the landlord, explaining that we were going on a late visit to an acquaintance, and that it was possible that we might spend the night there. A moment later we were out on the dark road, a chill wind blowing in our faces, and one yellow light twinkling in front of us through the gloom to guide us on our sombre errand.

There was little difficulty in entering the grounds, for unrepaired breaches gaped in the old park wall. Making our way among the trees, we reached the lawn, crossed it, and were about to enter through the window when out from a clump of laurel bushes there darted what seemed to be a hideous and distorted child, who threw itself upon the grass with writhing limbs and then ran swiftly across the lawn into the darkness.

'My God!' I whispered; 'did you see it?'

Holmes was for the moment as startled as I. His hand closed like a vice upon my wrist in his agitation. Then he broke into a low laugh and put his lips to my ear.

'It is a nice household,' he murmured. 'That is the baboon.'

I had forgotten the strange pets which the doctor affected. There was a cheetah, too; perhaps we might find it upon our shoulders at any moment. I confess that I felt easier in my mind when, after following Holmes' example and slipping off my shoes, I found myself inside the bedroom. My companion noiselessly closed the shutters, moved the lamp onto the table, and cast his eyes round the room. All was as we had seen it in the daytime. Then creeping up to me and making a trumpet of his hand, he whispered into my ear again so gently that it was all that I could do to distinguish the words:

'The least sound would be fatal to our plans.'

I nodded to show that I had heard.

'We must sit without light. He would see it through the ventilator.'

I nodded again.

'Do not go asleep; your very life may depend upon it. Have your pistol ready in case we should need it. I will sit on the side of the bed, and you in that chair.'

I took out my revolver and laid it on the corner of the table.

Holmes had brought up a long thin cane, and this he placed upon the bed beside him. By it he laid the box of matches and the stump of a candle. Then he turned down the lamp, and we were left in darkness.

How shall I ever forget that dreadful vigil? I could not hear a sound, not even the drawing of a breath, and yet I knew that my companion sat open-eyed, within a few feet of me, in the same state of nervous tension in which I was myself. The shutters cut off the least ray of light, and we waited in absolute darkness.

From outside came the occasional cry of a night-bird, and once at our very window a long-drawn cat-like whine, which told us that the cheetah was indeed at liberty. Far away we could hear the deep tones of the parish clock, which boomed out every quarter of an hour. How long they seemed, those quarters! Twelve struck, and one and two and three, and still we sat waiting silently for whatever might befall.

Suddenly there was the momentary gleam of a light up in the direction of the ventilator, which vanished immediately, but was succeeded by a strong smell of burning oil and heated metal. Someone in the next room had lit a dark-lantern. I heard a gentle sound of movement, and then all was silent once more, though the smell grew stronger. For half an hour I sat with straining ears. Then suddenly another sound became audible—a very gentle, soothing sound, like that of a small jet of steam escaping continually from a kettle. The instant that we heard it, Holmes sprang from the bed, struck a match, and lashed furiously with his cane at the bell-pull.

'You see it, Watson?' he yelled. 'You see it?'

But I saw nothing. At the moment when Holmes struck the light I heard a low, clear whistle, but the sudden glare flashing into my weary eyes made it impossible for me to tell what it was at which my friend lashed so savagely. I could, however, see that his face was deadly pale and filled with horror and loathing. He had ceased to strike and was gazing up at the ventilator when suddenly there broke from the silence of the night the most horrible cry to which I have ever listened. It swelled up louder and louder, a hoarse yell of pain and fear and anger all mingled in the one dreadful shriek. They say that away down in the village, and even in the distant parsonage, that cry raised the sleepers from their beds. It struck cold to our hearts, and I stood gazing at Holmes, and he at me, until the last echoes of it had died away into the silence from which it rose.

'What can it mean?' I gasped.

'It means that it is all over,' Holmes answered. 'And perhaps, after all, it is for the best. Take your pistol, and we will enter Dr Roylott's room.'

With a grave face he lit the lamp and led the way down the corridor. Twice he struck at the chamber door without any reply from within. Then he turned the handle and entered, I at his heels, with the cocked pistol in my hand.

It was a singular sight which met our eyes. On the table stood a dark-lantern with the shutter half open, throwing a brilliant beam of light upon the iron safe, the door of which was ajar. Beside this table, on the wooden chair, sat Dr Grimesby Roylott clad in a long grey dressing-gown, his bare ankles protruding beneath, and his feet thrust into red heelless Turkish slippers. Across his lap lay the short stock with the long lash which we had noticed during the day. His chin was cocked upward and his eyes were fixed in a dreadful, rigid stare at the corner of the ceiling. Round his brow he had a peculiar yellow band, with brownish speckles, which seemed to be bound tightly round his head. As we entered he made neither sound nor motion.

'The band! the speckled band!' whispered Holmes.

I took a step forward. In an instant his strange headgear began to move, and there reared itself from among his hair the squat diamond-shaped head and puffed neck of a loathsome serpent.

'It is a swamp adder!' cried Holmes; 'the deadliest snake in India. He has died within ten seconds of being bitten. Violence does, in truth, recoil upon the violent, and the schemer falls into the pit which he digs for another. Let us thrust this creature back into its den, and we can then remove Miss Stoner to some place of shelter and let the county police know what has happened.'

As he spoke he drew the dog-whip swiftly from the dead man's lap, and throwing the noose round the reptile's neck he drew it from its horrid perch and, carrying it at arm's length, threw it into the iron safe, which he closed upon it.

Such are the true facts of the death of Dr Grimesby Roylott, of Stoke Moran. It is not necessary that I should prolong a narrative which has already run to too great a length by telling how we broke the sad news to the terrified girl, how we conveyed her by the morning train to the care of her good aunt at Harrow, of how the slow process of official inquiry came to the conclusion that the doctor met his fate while indiscreetly playing with a dangerous pet. The little which I had yet to learn of the case was told to me by Sherlock Holmes as we travelled back next day.

'I had,' said he, 'come to an entirely erroneous conclusion which shows, my dear Watson, how dangerous it always is to reason from insufficient data. The presence of the gipsies, and the use of the word "band", which was used by the poor girl, no doubt, to explain the appearance which she had caught a hurried glimpse of by the light of her match, were sufficient to put me upon an entirely wrong scent. I can only claim the merit that I instantly reconsidered my position when, however, it became clear to me that whatever danger threatened an occupant of the room could not come either from the window or the door. My attention was speedily drawn, as I have already remarked to you, to this ventilator, and to the bell-rope which hung down to the bed. The discovery that this was a dummy, and that the bed was clamped to the floor, instantly gave rise to the suspicion that the rope was there as a bridge for something passing through the hole and coming to the bed. The idea of a snake instantly occurred to me, and when I coupled it with my knowledge that the doctor was furnished with a supply of creatures from India, I felt that I was probably on the right track. The idea of using a form of poison which could not possibly be discovered by any chemical test was just such a one as would occur to a clever and ruthless man who had had an Eastern training. The rapidity with which such a poison would take effect would also, from his point of view, be an advantage. It would be a sharp-eyed coroner, indeed, who could distinguish the two little dark punctures which would show where the poison fangs had done their work. Then I thought of the whistle. Of course he must recall the snake before the morning light revealed it to the victim. He had trained it, probably by the use of the milk which we saw, to return to him when summoned. He would put it through this ventilator at the hour that he thought best, with the certainty that it would crawl down the rope and land on the bed. It might or might not bite the occupant, perhaps she might escape every night for a week, but sooner or later she must fall a victim.

'I had come to these conclusions before ever I had entered his room. An inspection of his chair showed me that he had been in the habit of standing on it, which of course would be necessary in order that he should reach the ventilator. The sight of the safe, the saucer of milk, and the loop of whipcord were enough to finally dispel any doubts which may have remained. The metallic clang heard by Miss Stoner was obviously caused by her stepfather hastily closing the door of his safe upon its terrible occupant. Having once made up my mind, you know the steps which I took in order to put the matter to the proof. I heard the creature hiss as I have no doubt that you did also, and I instantly lit the light and attacked it.'

'With the result of driving it through the ventilator.'

'And also with the result of causing it to turn upon its master at the other side. Some of the blows of my cane came home and roused its snakish temper, so that it flew upon the first person it saw. In this way I am no doubt indirectly responsible for Dr Grimesby Roylott's death, and I cannot say that it is likely to weigh very heavily upon my conscience.'

the red-headed league

I had called upon my friend, Mr Sherlock Holmes, one day in the autumn of last year and found him in deep conversation with a very stout, florid-faced, elderly gentleman with fiery red hair. With an apology for my intrusion, I was about to withdraw when Holmes pulled me abruptly into the room and closed the door behind me.

'You could not possibly have come at a better time, my dear Watson,' he said cordially.

'I was afraid that you were engaged.'

'So I am. Very much so.'

'Then I can wait in the next room.'

'Not at all. This gentleman, Mr Wilson, has been my partner and helper in many of my most successful cases, and I have no doubt that he will be of the utmost use to me in yours also.'

The stout gentleman half rose from his chair and gave a bob of greeting, with a quick little questioning glance from his small fat-encircled eyes.

'Try the settee,' said Holmes, relapsing into his armchair

and putting his fingertips together, as was his custom when in judicial moods. 'I know, my dear Watson, that you share my love of all that is bizarre and outside the conventions and humdrum routine of everyday life. You have shown your relish for it by the enthusiasm which has prompted you to chronicle, and, if you will excuse my saying so, somewhat to embellish so many of my own little adventures.'

'Your cases have indeed been of the greatest interest to me,' I observed.

'You will remember that I remarked the other day, just before we went into the very simple problem presented by Miss Mary Sutherland, that for strange effects and extraordinary combinations we must go to life itself, which is always far more daring than any effort of the imagination.'

'A proposition which I took the liberty of doubting.'

'You did, Doctor, but nonetheless you must come round to my view, for otherwise I shall keep on piling fact upon fact on you until your reason breaks down under them and acknowledges me to be right. Now, Mr Jabez Wilson here has been good enough to call upon me this morning, and to begin a narrative which promises to be one of the most singular which I have listened to for some time. You have heard me remark that the strangest and most unique things are very often connected not with the larger but with the smaller crimes, and occasionally, indeed, where there is room for doubt whether any positive crime has been committed. As far as I have heard it is impossible for me to say whether the present case is an instance of crime or not, but the course of events is certainly among the most singular that I have ever listened to. Perhaps, Mr Wilson, you would have the great kindness to recommence your narrative. I ask you not merely because my friend Dr Watson has not heard the opening part but also because the peculiar nature of the story makes me anxious to have every possible detail from your lips. As a rule, when I have heard some slight indication of the course of events, I am able to guide myself by the thousands of other similar cases which occur to my memory. In the present instance I am forced to admit that the facts are, to the best of my belief, unique.'

The portly client puffed out his chest with an appearance of some little pride and pulled a dirty and wrinkled newspaper from the inside pocket of his greatcoat. As he glanced down the advertisement column, with his head thrust forward and the paper flattened out upon his knee, I took a good look at the man and endeavoured, after the fashion of my companion, to read the indications which might be presented by his dress or appearance.

I did not gain very much, however, by my inspection. Our visitor bore every mark of being an average commonplace British tradesman, obese, pompous, and slow. He wore rather baggy grey shepherd's check trousers, a not over-clean black frock-coat, unbuttoned in the front, and a drab waistcoat with a heavy brassy Albert chain, and a square pierced bit of metal dangling down as an ornament. A frayed top-hat and a faded brown overcoat with a wrinkled velvet collar lay upon a chair beside him. Altogether, look as

I would, there was nothing remarkable about the man save his blazing red head, and the expression of extreme chagrin and discontent upon his features.

Sherlock Holmes' quick eye took in my occupation, and he shook his head with a smile as he noticed my questioning glances. 'Beyond the obvious facts that he has at some time done manual labour, that he takes snuff, that he is a Freemason, that he has been in China, and that he has done a considerable amount of writing lately, I can deduce nothing else.'

Mr Jabez Wilson started up in his chair, with his forefinger upon the paper, but his eyes upon my companion.

'How, in the name of good-fortune, did you know all that, Mr Holmes?' he asked. 'How did you know, for example, that I did manual labour. It's as true as gospel, for I began as a ship's carpenter.'

'Your hands, my dear sir. Your right hand is quite a size larger than your left. You have worked with it, and the muscles are more developed.'

'Well, the snuff, then, and the Freemasonry?'

'I won't insult your intelligence by telling you how I read that, especially as, rather against the strict rules of your order, you use an arc-and-compass breastpin.'

'Ah, of course, I forgot that. But the writing?'

'What else can be indicated by that right cuff so very shiny for five inches, and the left one with the smooth patch near the elbow where you rest it upon the desk?'

'Well, but China?'

'The fish that you have tattooed immediately above your right wrist could only have been done in China. I have made a small study of tattoo marks and have even contributed to the literature of the subject. That trick of staining the fishes' scales of a delicate pink is quite peculiar to China. When, in addition, I see a Chinese coin hanging from your watch-chain, the matter becomes even more simple.'

Mr Jabez Wilson laughed heavily. 'Well, I never!' said he. 'I thought at first that you had done something clever, but I see that there was nothing in it, after all.'

'I begin to think, Watson,' said Holmes, 'that I make a mistake in explaining. "Omne ignotum pro magnifico," you know, and my poor little reputation, such as it is, will suffer shipwreck if I am so candid. Can you not find the advertisement, Mr Wilson?'

'Yes, I have got it now,' he answered with his thick red finger planted halfway down the column. 'Here it is. This is what began it all. You just read it for yourself, sir.'

I took the paper from him and read as follows:

'TO THE RED-HEADED LEAGUE: On account of the bequest of the late Ezekiah Hopkins, of Lebanon, Pennsylvania, U.S.A., there is now another vacancy open which entitles a member of the League to a salary of 4 pounds a week for purely nominal services. All red-headed men who are sound in body and mind and above the age of twenty-one years, are eligible. Apply in person on Monday, at eleven o'clock, to Duncan Ross, at the offices of the League, 7 Pope's Court, Fleet Street.'

'What on earth does this mean?' I ejaculated after I had twice read over the extraordinary announcement.

Holmes chuckled and wriggled in his chair, as was his habit when in high spirits. 'It is a little off the beaten track, isn't it?' said he. 'And now, Mr Wilson, off you go at scratch and tell us all about yourself, your household, and the effect which this advertisement had upon your fortunes. You will first make a note, Doctor, of the paper and the date.'

'It is *The Morning Chronicle* of April 27, 1890. Just two months ago.'

'Very good. Now, Mr Wilson?'

'Well, it is just as I have been telling you, Mr Sherlock Holmes,' said Jabez Wilson, mopping his forehead; 'I have a small pawnbroker's business at Coburg Square, near the City. It's not a very large affair, and of late years it has not done more than just give me a living. I used to be able to keep two assistants, but now I only keep one; and I would have a job to pay him but that he is willing to come for half wages so as to learn the business.'

'What is the name of this obliging youth?' asked Sherlock Holmes.

'His name is Vincent Spaulding, and he's not such a youth, either. It's hard to say his age. I should not wish a smarter assistant, Mr Holmes; and I know very well that he could better himself and earn twice what I am able to give him. But, after all, if he is satisfied, why should I put ideas in his head?'

'Why, indeed? You seem most fortunate in having an employé who comes under the full market price. It is not a common experience among employers in this age. I don't know that your assistant is not as remarkable as your advertisement.'

'Oh, he has his faults, too,' said Mr Wilson. 'Never was such a fellow for photography. Snapping away with a camera when he ought to be improving his mind, and then diving down into the cellar like a rabbit into its hole to develop his pictures. That is his main fault, but on the whole he's a good worker. There's no vice in him.'

'He is still with you, I presume?'

'Yes, sir. He and a girl of fourteen, who does a bit of simple cooking and keeps the place clean—that's all I have in the house, for I am a widower and never had any family. We live very quietly, sir, the three of us; and we keep a roof over our heads and pay our debts, if we do nothing more.

'The first thing that put us out was that advertisement. Spaulding, he came down into the office just this day eight weeks, with this very paper in his hand, and he says:

'"I wish to the Lord, Mr Wilson, that I was a red-headed man."

'"Why is that?" I asked.

'"Why," says he, "here's another vacancy on the League of the Red-headed Men. It's worth quite a little fortune to any man who gets it, and I understand that there are more vacancies than there are men, so that the trustees are at their wits' end what to do with the money. If my hair would only change colour, here's a nice little crib all ready for me to step into."

"'Why, what is it, then?' I asked. You see, Mr Holmes, I am a very stay-at-home man, and as my business came to me instead of my having to go to it, I was often weeks on end without putting my foot over the door-mat. In that way I didn't know much of what was going on outside, and I was always glad of a bit of news.

"'Have you never heard of the League of the Red-headed Men?' he asked with his eyes open.

"'Never.'

"'Why, I wonder at that, for you are eligible yourself for one of the vacancies.'

"'And what are they worth?' I asked.

"'Oh, merely a couple of hundred a year, but the work is slight, and it need not interfere very much with one's other occupations.'

'Well, you can easily think that that made me prick up my ears, for the business has not been over-good for some years, and an extra couple of hundred would have been very handy.

"'Tell me all about it,' said I.

"'Well,' said he, showing me the advertisement, "you can see for yourself that the League has a vacancy, and there is the address where you should apply for particulars. As far as I can make out, the League was founded by an American millionaire, Ezekiah Hopkins, who was very peculiar in his ways. He was himself red-headed, and he had a great sympathy for all red-headed men; so when he died it was found that he had left his enormous fortune in the hands of trustees, with instructions to apply the interest to the providing of easy berths to men whose hair is of that colour. From all I hear it is splendid pay and very little to do."

'"But," said I, "there would be millions of red-headed men who would apply."

'"Not so many as you might think," he answered. "You see it is really confined to Londoners, and to grown men. This American had started from London when he was young, and he wanted to do the old town a good turn. Then, again, I have heard it is no use your applying if your hair is light red, or dark red, or anything but real bright, blazing, fiery red. Now, if you cared to apply, Mr Wilson, you would just walk in; but perhaps it would hardly be worth your while to put yourself out of the way for the sake of a few hundred pounds."

'Now, it is a fact, gentlemen, as you may see for yourselves, that my hair is of a very full and rich tint, so that it seemed to me that if there was to be any competition in the matter I stood as good a chance as any man that I had ever met. Vincent Spaulding seemed to know so much about it that I thought he might prove useful, so I just ordered him to put up the shutters for the day and to come right away with me. He was very willing to have a holiday, so we shut the business up and started off for the address that was given us in the advertisement.

'I never hope to see such a sight as that again, Mr

Holmes. From north, south, east, and west every man who had a shade of red in his hair had tramped into the city to answer the advertisement. Fleet Street was choked with red-headed folk, and Pope's Court looked like a coster's orange barrow. I should not have thought there were so many in the whole country as were brought together by that single advertisement. Every shade of colour they were— straw, lemon, orange, brick, Irish-setter, liver, clay; but, as Spaulding said, there were not many who had the real vivid flame-coloured tint. When I saw how many were waiting, I would have given it up in despair; but Spaulding would not hear of it. How he did it I could not imagine, but he pushed and pulled and butted until he got me through the crowd, and right up to the steps which led to the office. There was a double stream upon the stair, some going up in hope, and some coming back dejected; but we wedged in as well as we could and soon found ourselves in the office.'

'Your experience has been a most entertaining one,' remarked Holmes as his client paused and refreshed his memory with a huge pinch of snuff. 'Pray continue your very interesting statement.'

'There was nothing in the office but a couple of wooden chairs and a deal table, behind which sat a small man with a head that was even redder than mine. He said a few words to each candidate as he came up, and then he always managed to find some fault in them which would disqualify them. Getting a vacancy did not seem to be such a very easy matter, after all. However, when our turn came the little man was much more favourable to me than to any of the others, and he closed the door as we entered, so that he might have a private word with us.

"'This is Mr Jabez Wilson,' said my assistant, 'and he is willing to fill a vacancy in the League.'

"'And he is admirably suited for it,' the other answered. "He has every requirement. I cannot recall when I have seen anything so fine.' He took a step backward, cocked his head on one side, and gazed at my hair until I felt quite bashful. Then suddenly he plunged forward, wrung my hand, and congratulated me warmly on my success.

"'It would be injustice to hesitate,' said he. "You will, however, I am sure, excuse me for taking an obvious precaution.' With that he seized my hair in both his hands, and tugged until I yelled with the pain. "There is water in your eyes,' said he as he released me. "I perceive that all is as it should be. But we have to be careful, for we have twice been deceived by wigs and once by paint. I could tell you tales of cobbler's wax which would disgust you with human nature.' He stepped over to the window and shouted through it at the top of his voice that the vacancy was filled. A groan of disappointment came up from below, and the folk all trooped away in different directions until there was not a red-head to be seen except my own and that of the manager.

"'My name,' said he, 'is Mr Duncan Ross, and I am myself one of the pensioners upon the fund left by our noble benefactor. Are you a married man, Mr Wilson? Have you a family?'"

'I answered that I had not.

'His face fell immediately.

'"Dear me!" he said gravely, "that is very serious indeed! I am sorry to hear you say that. The fund was, of course, for the propagation and spread of the red-heads as well as for their maintenance. It is exceedingly unfortunate that you should be a bachelor."

'My face lengthened at this, Mr Holmes, for I thought that I was not to have the vacancy after all; but after thinking it over for a few minutes he said that it would be all right.

'"In the case of another," said he, "the objection might be fatal, but we must stretch a point in favour of a man with such a head of hair as yours. When shall you be able to enter upon your new duties?"

'"Well, it is a little awkward, for I have a business already," said I.

'"Oh, never mind about that, Mr Wilson!" said Vincent Spaulding. "I should be able to look after that for you."

'"What would be the hours?" I asked.

'"Ten to two."

'Now a pawnbroker's business is mostly done of an evening, Mr Holmes, especially Thursday and Friday evening, which is just before pay-day; so it would suit me very well to earn a little in the mornings. Besides, I knew that my assistant was a good man, and that he would see to anything that turned up.

'"That would suit me very well," said I. "And the pay?"

'"Is 4 pounds a week."

'"And the work?"

"'Is purely nominal."

"'What do you call purely nominal?"

"'Well, you have to be in the office, or at least in the building, the whole time. If you leave, you forfeit your whole position forever. The will is very clear upon that point. You don't comply with the conditions if you budge from the office during that time."

"'It's only four hours a day, and I should not think of leaving," said I.

"'No excuse will avail," said Mr Duncan Ross; "neither sickness nor business nor anything else. There you must stay, or you lose your billet."

"'And the work?"

"'Is to copy out the *Encyclopaedia Britannica*. There is the first volume of it in that press. You must find your own ink, pens, and blotting-paper, but we provide this table and chair. Will you be ready to-morrow?"

"'Certainly," I answered.

"'Then, good-bye, Mr Jabez Wilson, and let me congratulate you once more on the important position which you have been fortunate enough to gain." He bowed me out of the room and I went home with my assistant, hardly knowing what to say or do, I was so pleased at my own good fortune.

'Well, I thought over the matter all day, and by evening I was in low spirits again; for I had quite persuaded myself that the whole affair must be some great hoax or fraud, though what its object might be I could not imagine. It seemed altogether past belief that anyone could make such a will, or that they would pay such a sum for doing anything so simple as copying out the *Encyclopaedia Britannica*. Vincent Spaulding did what he could to cheer me up, but by bedtime I had reasoned myself out of the whole thing. However, in the morning I determined to have a look at it anyhow, so I bought a penny bottle of ink, and with a quill-pen, and seven sheets of foolscap paper, I started off for Pope's Court.

'Well, to my surprise and delight, everything was as right as possible. The table was set out ready for me, and Mr Duncan Ross was there to see that I got fairly to work. He started me off upon the letter A, and then he left me; but he would drop in from time to time to see that all was right with me. At two o'clock he bade me good-day, complimented me upon the amount that I had written, and locked the door of the office after me.

'This went on day after day, Mr Holmes, and on Saturday the manager came in and planked down four golden sovereigns for my week's work. It was the same next week, and the same the week after. Every morning I was there at ten, and every afternoon I left at two. By degrees Mr Duncan Ross took to coming in only once of a morning, and then, after a time, he did not come in at all. Still, of course, I never dared to leave the room for an instant, for I was not sure when he might come, and the billet was such a good one, and suited me so well, that I would not risk the loss of it.

'Eight weeks passed away like this, and I had written about Abbots and Archery and Armour and Architecture and Attica, and hoped with diligence that I might get on to the B's before very long. It cost me something in foolscap, and I had pretty nearly filled a shelf with my writings. And then suddenly the whole business came to an end.'

'To an end?'

'Yes, sir. And no later than this morning. I went to my work as usual at ten o'clock, but the door was shut and locked, with a little square of cardboard hammered on to the middle of the panel with a tack. Here it is, and you can read for yourself.'

He held up a piece of white cardboard about the size of a sheet of note-paper. It read in this fashion:

THE RED-HEADED LEAGUE

IS

DISSOLVED.

October 9, 1890.

Sherlock Holmes and I surveyed this curt announcement and the rueful face behind it, until the comical side of the affair so completely overtopped every other consideration that we both burst out into a roar of laughter.

'I cannot see that there is anything very funny,' cried our client, flushing up to the roots of his flaming head. 'If you can do nothing better than laugh at me, I can go elsewhere.'

'No, no,' cried Holmes, shoving him back into the chair from which he had half-risen. 'I really wouldn't miss your case for the world. It is most refreshingly unusual. But there is, if you will excuse my saying so, something just a little funny about it. Pray what steps did you take when you found the card upon the door?'

'I was staggered, sir. I did not know what to do. Then I called at the offices round, but none of them seemed to know anything about it. Finally, I went to the landlord, who is an accountant living on the ground-floor, and I asked him if he could tell me what had become of the Red-headed League. He said that he had never heard of any such body. Then I asked him who Mr Duncan Ross was. He answered that the name was new to him.

'"Well," said I, "the gentleman at No. 4."

'"What, the red-headed man?"

'"Yes."

'"Oh," said he, "his name was William Morris. He was a solicitor and was using my room as a temporary convenience until his new premises were ready. He moved out yesterday."

'"Where could I find him?"

'"Oh, at his new offices. He did tell me the address. Yes, 17 King Edward Street, near St Paul's."

'I started off, Mr Holmes, but when I got to that address it was a manufactory of artificial knee-caps, and no one in it had ever heard of either Mr William Morris or Mr Duncan Ross.'

'And what did you do then?' asked Holmes.

'I went home to Saxe-Coburg Square, and I took the advice of my assistant. But he could not help me in any way. He could only say that if I waited I should hear by post. But that was not quite good enough, Mr Holmes. I did not wish to lose such a place without a struggle, so, as I had heard that you were good enough to give advice to poor folk who were in need of it, I came right away to you.'

'And you did very wisely,' said Holmes. 'Your case is an exceedingly remarkable one, and I shall be happy to look into it. From what you have told me I think that it is possible that graver issues hang from it than might at first sight appear.'

'Grave enough!' said Mr Jabez Wilson. 'Why, I have lost four pounds a week.'

'As far as you are personally concerned,' remarked Holmes, 'I do not see that you have any grievance against this extraordinary league. On the contrary, you are, as I understand, richer by some 30 pounds, to say nothing of the minute knowledge which you have gained on every subject which comes under the letter A. You have lost nothing by them.'

'No, sir. But I want to find out about them, and who they are, and what their object was in playing this prank— if it was a prank—upon me. It was a pretty expensive joke for them, for it cost them two and thirty pounds.'

'We shall endeavour to clear up these points for you. And, first, one or two questions, Mr Wilson. This assistant of yours who first called your attention to the advertisement— how long had he been with you?'

'About a month then.'

'How did he come?'

'In answer to an advertisement.'

'Was he the only applicant?'

'No, I had a dozen.'

'Why did you pick him?'

'Because he was handy and would come cheap.'

'At half-wages, in fact.'

'Yes.'

'What is he like, this Vincent Spaulding?'

'Small, stout-built, very quick in his ways, no hair on his face, though he's not short of thirty. Has a white splash of acid upon his forehead.'

Holmes sat up in his chair in considerable excitement. 'I thought as much,' said he. 'Have you ever observed that his ears are pierced for earrings?'

'Yes, sir. He told me that a gipsy had done it for him when he was a lad.'

'Hum!' said Holmes, sinking back in deep thought. 'He is still with you?'

'Oh, yes, sir; I have only just left him.'

'And has your business been attended to in your absence?'

'Nothing to complain of, sir. There's never very much to do of a morning.'

'That will do, Mr Wilson. I shall be happy to give you an opinion upon the subject in the course of a day or two. To-day is Saturday, and I hope that by Monday we may come to a conclusion.'

'Well, Watson,' said Holmes when our visitor had left us, 'what do you make of it all?'

'I make nothing of it,' I answered frankly. 'It is a most mysterious business.'

'As a rule,' said Holmes, 'the more bizarre a thing is the less mysterious it proves to be. It is your commonplace, featureless crimes which are really puzzling, just as a commonplace face is the most difficult to identify. But I must be prompt over this matter.'

'What are you going to do, then?' I asked.

'To smoke,' he answered. 'It is quite a three pipe problem, and I beg that you won't speak to me for fifty minutes.' He curled himself up in his chair, with his thin knees drawn up to his hawk-like nose, and there he sat with his eyes closed and his black clay pipe thrusting out like the bill of some strange bird. I had come to the conclusion that he had dropped asleep, and indeed was nodding myself, when he suddenly sprang out of his chair with the gesture of a man who has made up his mind and put his pipe down upon the mantelpiece.

'Sarasate plays at the St James's Hall this afternoon,' he remarked. 'What do you think, Watson? Could your patients spare you for a few hours?'

'I have nothing to do to-day. My practice is never very absorbing.'

'Then put on your hat and come. I am going through the city first, and we can have some lunch on the way. I observe that there is a good deal of German music on the programme, which is rather more to my taste than Italian or French. It is introspective, and I want to introspect. Come along!'

We travelled by the Underground as far as Aldersgate, and a short walk took us to Saxe-Coburg Square, the scene of the singular story which we had listened to in the morning. It was a poky, little, shabby-genteel place, where four lines of dingy two-storied brick houses looked out into a small railed-in enclosure, where a lawn of weedy grass and a few clumps of faded laurel bushes made a hard fight against a smoke-laden and uncongenial atmosphere. Three gilt balls and a brown board with 'JABEZ WILSON' in white letters, upon a corner house, announced the place where our red-headed client carried on his business. Sherlock Holmes stopped in front of it with his head on one side and looked it all over, with his eyes shining brightly between puckered lids. Then he walked slowly up the street, and then down again to the corner, still looking keenly at the houses. Finally he returned to the pawnbroker's, and, having thumped vigorously upon the pavement with his stick two or three times, he went up to the door and knocked. It was instantly opened by a bright-looking, clean-shaven young fellow, who asked him to step in.

'Thank you,' said Holmes, 'I only wished to ask you how you would go from here to the Strand.'

'Third right, fourth left,' answered the assistant promptly, closing the door.

'Smart fellow, that,' observed Holmes as we walked away. 'He is, in my judgment, the fourth smartest man in London, and for daring I am not sure that he has not a claim to be third. I have known something of him before.'

'Evidently,' said I, 'Mr Wilson's assistant counts for a good deal in this mystery of the Red-headed League. I am sure that you inquired your way merely in order that you might see him.'

'Not him.'

'What then?'

'The knees of his trousers.'

'And what did you see?'

'What I expected to see.'

'Why did you beat the pavement?'

'My dear doctor, this is a time for observation, not for talk. We are spies in an enemy's country. We know something of Saxe-Coburg Square. Let us now explore the parts which lie behind it.'

The road in which we found ourselves as we turned round the corner from the retired Saxe-Coburg Square presented as great a contrast to it as the front of a picture does to the back. It was one of the main arteries which conveyed the traffic of the City to the north and west. The roadway was blocked with the immense stream of commerce flowing in a double tide inward and outward, while the footpaths were black with the hurrying swarm of pedestrians. It was difficult to realize as we looked at the line of fine shops and stately business premises that they really abutted on the other side upon the faded and stagnant square which we had just quitted.

'Let me see,' said Holmes, standing at the corner and glancing along the line, 'I should like just to remember the order of the houses here. It is a hobby of mine to have an exact knowledge of London. There is Mortimer's, the tobacconist, the little newspaper shop, the Coburg branch of the City and Suburban Bank, the Vegetarian Restaurant, and McFarlane's carriage-building depot. That carries us right on to the other block. And now, Doctor, we've done our work, so it's time we had some play. A sandwich and a cup of coffee, and then off to violin-land, where all is sweetness and delicacy and harmony, and there are no red-headed clients to vex us with their conundrums.'

My friend was an enthusiastic musician, being himself not only a very capable performer but a composer of no ordinary merit. All the afternoon he sat in the stalls wrapped in the most perfect happiness, gently waving his long, thin fingers in time to the music, while his gently smiling face and his languid, dreamy eyes were as unlike those of Holmes the sleuth-hound, Holmes the relentless, keen-witted, ready-handed criminal agent, as it was possible to conceive. In his singular character the dual nature alternately asserted itself, and his extreme exactness and astuteness represented, as I have often thought, the reaction against the poetic and contemplative mood which occasionally predominated in him. The swing of his nature took him from extreme languor to devouring energy; and, as I knew well, he was never so truly formidable as when, for days on end, he had been lounging in his armchair amid his improvisations and his black-letter editions. Then it was that the lust of the chase would suddenly come upon him, and that his brilliant reasoning power would rise to the level of intuition, until those who were unacquainted with his methods would look askance at him as on a man whose knowledge was not that of other mortals. When I saw him that afternoon so enwrapped in the music at St James's Hall I felt that an evil time might be coming upon those whom he had set himself to hunt down.

'You want to go home, no doubt, Doctor,' he remarked as we emerged.

'Yes, it would be as well.'

'And I have some business to do which will take some hours. This business at Coburg Square is serious.'

'Why serious?'

'A considerable crime is in contemplation. I have every reason to believe that we shall be in time to stop it. But to-day being Saturday rather complicates matters. I shall want your help to-night.'

'At what time?'

'Ten will be early enough.'

'I shall be at Baker Street at ten.'

'Very well. And, I say, Doctor, there may be some little danger, so kindly put your army revolver in your pocket.' He waved his hand, turned on his heel, and disappeared in an instant among the crowd.

I trust that I am not more dense than my neighbours, but I was always oppressed with a sense of my own stupidity in my dealings with Sherlock Holmes. Here I had heard what he had heard, I had seen what he had seen, and yet from his words it was evident that he saw clearly not only what had happened but what was about to happen, while to me the whole business was still confused and grotesque. As I drove home to my house in Kensington I thought over it all, from the extraordinary story of the red-headed copier of the *Encyclopaedia* down to the visit to Saxe-Coburg Square, and the ominous words with which he had parted from me. What was this nocturnal expedition, and why should I go armed? Where were we going, and what were we to do? I had the hint from Holmes that this smooth-faced pawnbroker's assistant was a formidable man—a man who might play a deep game. I tried to puzzle it out, but gave it up in despair and set the matter aside until night should bring an explanation.

It was a quarter-past nine when I started from home and made my way across the Park, and so through Oxford Street to Baker Street. Two hansoms were standing at the door, and as I entered the passage I heard the sound of voices from above. On entering his room I found Holmes in animated conversation with two men, one of whom I recognized as Peter Jones, the official police agent, while the other was a long, thin, sad-faced man, with a very shiny hat and oppressively respectable frock-coat.

'Ha! Our party is complete,' said Holmes, buttoning up his pea-jacket and taking his heavy hunting crop from the rack. 'Watson, I think you know Mr Jones, of Scotland Yard? Let me introduce you to Mr Merryweather, who is to be our companion in to-night's adventure.'

'We're hunting in couples again, Doctor, you see,' said Jones in his consequential way. 'Our friend here is a wonderful man for starting a chase. All he wants is an old dog to help him to do the running down.'

'I hope a wild goose may not prove to be the end of our chase,' observed Mr Merryweather gloomily.

'You may place considerable confidence in Mr Holmes, sir,' said the police agent loftily. 'He has his own little methods, which are, if he won't mind my saying so, just a little too theoretical and fantastic, but he has the makings of a detective in him. It is not too much to say that once or twice, as in that business of the Sholto murder and the Agra treasure, he has been more nearly correct than the official force.'

'Oh, if you say so, Mr Jones, it is all right,' said the stranger with deference. 'Still, I confess that I miss my rubber. It is the first Saturday night for seven-and-twenty years that I have not had my rubber.'

'I think you will find,' said Sherlock Holmes, 'that you will play for a higher stake to-night than you have ever done yet, and that the play will be more exciting. For you, Mr Merryweather, the stake will be some 30,000 pounds; and for you, Jones, it will be the man upon whom you wish to lay your hands.'

'John Clay, the murderer, thief, smasher, and forger. He's a young man, Mr Merryweather, but he is at the head of his profession, and I would rather have my bracelets on him than on any criminal in London. He's a remarkable man, is young John Clay. His grandfather was a royal duke, and he himself has been to Eton and Oxford. His brain is as cunning as his fingers, and though we meet signs of him at every turn, we never know where to find the man himself. He'll crack a crib in Scotland one week, and be raising money to build an orphanage in Cornwall the next. I've been on his track for years and have never set eyes on him yet.'

'I hope that I may have the pleasure of introducing you to-night. I've had one or two little turns also with Mr John Clay, and I agree with you that he is at the head of his profession. It is past ten, however, and quite time that we started. If you two will take the first hansom, Watson and I will follow in the second.'

Sherlock Holmes was not very communicative during the long drive and lay back in the cab humming the tunes which he had heard in the afternoon. We rattled through an endless labyrinth of gas-lit streets until we emerged into Farrington Street.

'We are close there now,' my friend remarked. 'This fellow Merryweather is a bank director, and personally interested in the matter. I thought it as well to have Jones with us also. He is not a bad fellow, though an absolute imbecile in his profession. He has one positive virtue. He is as brave as a bulldog and as tenacious as a lobster if he gets his claws upon anyone. Here we are, and they are waiting for us.'

We had reached the same crowded thoroughfare in which we had found ourselves in the morning. Our cabs were dismissed, and, following the guidance of Mr Merryweather, we passed down a narrow passage and through a side door, which he opened for us. Within there was a small corridor, which ended in a very massive iron gate. This also was opened, and led down a flight of winding stone steps, which terminated at another formidable gate. Mr Merryweather stopped to light a lantern, and then conducted us down a dark, earth-smelling passage, and so, after opening a third door, into a huge vault or cellar, which was piled all round with crates and massive boxes.

'You are not very vulnerable from above,' Holmes remarked as he held up the lantern and gazed about him.

'Nor from below,' said Mr Merryweather, striking his stick upon the flags which lined the floor. 'Why, dear me, it sounds quite hollow!' he remarked, looking up in surprise.

'I must really ask you to be a little more quiet!' said Holmes severely. 'You have already imperilled the whole success of our expedition. Might I beg that you would have the goodness to sit down upon one of those boxes, and not to interfere?'

The solemn Mr Merryweather perched himself upon a crate, with a very injured expression upon his face, while Holmes fell upon his knees upon the floor and, with the lantern and a magnifying lens, began to examine minutely the cracks between the stones. A few seconds sufficed to satisfy him, for he sprang to his feet again and put his glass in his pocket.

'We have at least an hour before us,' he remarked, 'for they can hardly take any steps until the good pawnbroker is safely in bed. Then they will not lose a minute, for the sooner they do their work the longer time they will have for their escape. We are at present, Doctor—as no doubt you have divined—in the cellar of the City branch of one of the principal London banks. Mr Merryweather is the chairman of directors, and he will explain to you that there are reasons why the more daring criminals of London should take a considerable interest in this cellar at present.'

'It is our French gold,' whispered the director. 'We have had several warnings that an attempt might be made upon it.'

'Your French gold?'

'Yes. We had occasion some months ago to strengthen our resources and borrowed for that purpose 30,000 napoleons from the Bank of France. It has become known that we have never had occasion to unpack the money, and that it is still lying in our cellar. The crate upon which I sit contains 2,000 napoleons packed between layers of lead foil. Our reserve of bullion is much larger at present than is usually kept in a single branch office, and the directors have had misgivings upon the subject.'

'Which were very well justified,' observed Holmes. 'And now it is time that we arranged our little plans. I expect that within an hour matters will come to a head. In the meantime Mr Merryweather, we must put the screen over that dark lantern.'

'And sit in the dark?'

'I am afraid so. I had brought a pack of cards in my pocket, and I thought that, as we were a partie carrée, you might have your rubber after all. But I see that the enemy's preparations have gone so far that we cannot risk the presence of a light. And, first of all, we must choose our positions. These are daring men, and though we shall take them at a disadvantage, they may do us some harm unless we are careful. I shall stand behind this crate, and you conceal yourselves behind those. Then, when I flash a light upon them, close in swiftly. If they fire, Watson, have no compunction about shooting them down.'

I placed my revolver, cocked, upon the top of the wooden case behind which I crouched. Holmes shot the slide across the front of his lantern and left us in pitch darkness—such an absolute darkness as I have never before experienced. The smell of hot metal remained to assure us that the light was still there, ready to flash out at a moment's notice. To me, with my nerves worked up to a pitch of expectancy, there was something depressing and subduing in the sudden gloom, and in the cold dank air of the vault.

'They have but one retreat,' whispered Holmes. 'That is back through the house into Saxe-Coburg Square. I hope that you have done what I asked you, Jones?'

'I have an inspector and two officers waiting at the front door.'

'Then we have stopped all the holes. And now we must be silent and wait.'

What a time it seemed! From comparing notes afterwards it was but an hour and a quarter, yet it appeared to me that the night must have almost gone and the dawn be breaking above us. My limbs were weary and stiff, for I feared to change my position; yet my nerves were worked up to the highest pitch of tension, and my hearing was so acute that I could not only hear the gentle breathing of my companions, but I could distinguish the deeper, heavier in-breath of the bulky Jones from the thin, sighing note of the bank director. From my position I could look over the case in the direction of the floor. Suddenly my eyes caught the glint of a light.

At first it was but a lurid spark upon the stone pavement. Then it lengthened out until it became a yellow line, and then, without any warning or sound, a gash seemed to open and a hand appeared, a white, almost womanly hand, which felt about in the centre of the little area of light. For a minute or more the hand, with its writhing fingers, protruded out of the floor. Then it was withdrawn as suddenly as it appeared, and all was dark again save the single lurid spark which marked a chink between the stones.

Its disappearance, however, was but momentary. With a rending, tearing sound, one of the broad, white stones turned over upon its side and left a square, gaping hole, through which streamed the light of a lantern. Over the edge there peeped a clean-cut, boyish face, which looked keenly about it, and then, with a hand on either side of the aperture, drew itself shoulder-high and waist-high, until one knee rested upon the edge. In another instant he stood at the side of the hole and was hauling after him a companion, lithe and small like himself, with a pale face and a shock of very red hair.

'It's all clear,' he whispered. 'Have you the chisel and the bags? Great Scott! Jump, Archie, jump, and I'll swing for it!'

Sherlock Holmes had sprung out and seized the intruder

by the collar. The other dived down the hole, and I heard the sound of rending cloth as Jones clutched at his skirts. The light flashed upon the barrel of a revolver, but Holmes' hunting crop came down on the man's wrist, and the pistol clinked upon the stone floor.

'It's no use, John Clay,' said Holmes blandly. 'You have no chance at all.'

'So I see,' the other answered with the utmost coolness. 'I fancy that my pal is all right, though I see you have got his coat-tails.'

'There are three men waiting for him at the door,' said Holmes.

'Oh, indeed! You seem to have done the thing very completely. I must compliment you.'

'And I you,' Holmes answered. 'Your red-headed idea was very new and effective.'

'You'll see your pal again presently,' said Jones. 'He's quicker at climbing down holes than I am. Just hold out while I fix the derbies.'

'I beg that you will not touch me with your filthy hands,' remarked our prisoner as the handcuffs clattered upon his wrists. 'You may not be aware that I have royal blood in my veins. Have the goodness, also, when you address me always to say "sir" and "please".'

'All right,' said Jones with a stare and a snigger. 'Well, would you please, sir, march upstairs, where we can get a cab to carry your Highness to the police-station?'

'That is better,' said John Clay serenely. He made a

sweeping bow to the three of us and walked quietly off in the custody of the detective.

'Really, Mr Holmes,' said Mr Merryweather as we followed them from the cellar, 'I do not know how the bank can thank you or repay you. There is no doubt that you have detected and defeated in the most complete manner one of the most determined attempts at bank robbery that have ever come within my experience.'

'I have had one or two little scores of my own to settle with Mr John Clay,' said Holmes. 'I have been at some small expense over this matter, which I shall expect the bank to refund, but beyond that I am amply repaid by having had an experience which is in many ways unique, and by hearing the very remarkable narrative of the Red-headed League.'

'You see, Watson,' he explained in the early hours of the morning as we sat over a glass of whisky and soda in Baker Street, 'it was perfectly obvious from the first that the only possible object of this rather fantastic business of the advertisement of the League, and the copying of the *Encyclopaedia*, must be to get this not over-bright pawnbroker out of the way for a number of hours every day. It was a curious way of managing it, but, really, it would be difficult to suggest a better. The method was no doubt suggested to Clay's ingenious mind by the colour of his accomplice's hair. The 4 pounds a week was a lure which must draw him, and what was it to them, who were playing for thousands? They put in the advertisement, one rogue has the temporary office, the other rogue incites the man to apply for it, and together they manage to secure his absence every morning in the week. From the time that I heard of the assistant having come for half wages, it was obvious to me that he had some strong motive for securing the situation.'

'But how could you guess what the motive was?'

'Had there been women in the house, I should have suspected a mere vulgar intrigue. That, however, was out of the question. The man's business was a small one, and there was nothing in his house which could account for such elaborate preparations, and such an expenditure as they were at. It must, then, be something out of the house. What could it be? I thought of the assistant's fondness for photography, and his trick of vanishing into the cellar. The cellar! There was the end of this tangled clue. Then I made inquiries as to this mysterious assistant and found that I had to deal with one of the coolest and most daring criminals in London. He was doing something in the cellar—something which took many hours a day for months on end. What could it be, once more? I could think of nothing save that he was running a tunnel to some other building.

'So far I had got when we went to visit the scene of action. I surprised you by beating upon the pavement with my stick. I was ascertaining whether the cellar stretched out in front or behind. It was not in front. Then I rang the bell, and, as I hoped, the assistant answered it. We have had some skirmishes, but we had never set eyes upon each other before. I hardly looked at his face. His knees were what I wished to see. You must yourself have remarked how worn, wrinkled, and stained they were. They spoke of those hours of burrowing. The only remaining point was what they were burrowing for. I walked round the corner, saw the City and Suburban Bank abutted on our friend's premises, and felt that I had solved my problem. When you drove home after the concert I called upon Scotland Yard and upon the chairman of the bank directors, with the result that you have seen.'

'And how could you tell that they would make their attempt to-night?' I asked.

'Well, when they closed their League offices that was a sign that they cared no longer about Mr Jabez Wilson's presence—in other words, that they had completed their tunnel. But it was essential that they should use it soon, as it might be discovered, or the bullion might be removed. Saturday would suit them better than any other day, as it would give them two days for their escape. For all these reasons I expected them to come to-night.'

'You reasoned it out beautifully,' I exclaimed in unfeigned admiration. 'It is so long a chain, and yet every link rings true.'

'It saved me from ennui,' he answered, yawning. 'Alas! I already feel it closing in upon me. My life is spent in one long effort to escape from the commonplaces of existence. These little problems help me to do so.'

'And you are a benefactor of the race,' said I.

He shrugged his shoulders. 'Well, perhaps, after all, it is of some little use,' he remarked. '"L'homme c'est rien—l'oeuvre c'est tout," as Gustave Flaubert wrote to George Sand.'

the adventure of the dancing men

Holmes had been seated for some hours in silence with his long, thin back curved over a chemical vessel in which he was brewing a particularly malodorous product. His head was sunk upon his breast, and he looked from my point of view like a strange, lank bird, with dull grey plumage and a black top-knot.

'So, Watson,' said he, suddenly, 'you do not propose to invest in South African securities?'

I gave a start of astonishment. Accustomed as I was to Holmes' curious faculties, this sudden intrusion into my most intimate thoughts was utterly inexplicable.

'How on earth do you know that?' I asked.

He wheeled round upon his stool, with a steaming test-tube in his hand, and a gleam of amusement in his deep-set eyes.

'Now, Watson, confess yourself utterly taken aback,' said he.

'I am.'

'I ought to make you sign a paper to that effect.'

'Why?'

'Because in five minutes you will say that it is all so absurdly simple.'

'I am sure that I shall say nothing of the kind.'

'You see, my dear Watson'—he propped his test-tube in the rack, and began to lecture with the air of a professor addressing his class—'it is not really difficult to construct a series of inferences, each dependent upon its predecessor and each simple in itself. If, after doing so, one simply knocks out all the central inferences and presents one's audience with the starting-point and the conclusion, one may produce a startling, though possibly a meretricious, effect. Now, it was not really difficult, by an inspection of the groove between your left forefinger and thumb, to feel sure that you did *not* propose to invest your small capital in the goldfields.'

'I see no connection.'

'Very likely not; but I can quickly show you a close connection. Here are the missing links of the very simple chain: 1. You had chalk between your left finger and thumb when you returned from the club last night. 2. You put chalk there when you play billiards to steady the cue. 3. You never play billiards except with Thurston. 4. You told me, four weeks ago, that Thurston had an option on some South African property which would expire in a month, and which he desired you to share with him. 5. Your cheque-book is locked in my drawer, and you have not asked for the key. 6. You do not propose to invest your money in this manner.'

'How absurdly simple!' I cried.

'Quite so!' said he, a little nettled. 'Every problem becomes very childish when once it is explained to you. Here is an unexplained one. See what you can make of that, friend Watson.' He tossed a sheet of paper upon the table, and turned once more to his chemical analysis.

I looked with amazement at the absurd hieroglyphics upon the paper.

'Why, Holmes, it is a child's drawing,' I cried.

'Oh, that's your idea!'

'What else should it be?'

'That is what Mr Hilton Cubitt, of Riding Thorpe Manor, Norfolk, is very anxious to know. This little conundrum came by the first post, and he was to follow by the next train. There's a ring at the bell, Watson. I should not be very much surprised if this were he.'

A heavy step was heard upon the stairs, and an instant later there entered a tall, ruddy, clean-shaven gentleman, whose clear eyes and florid cheeks told of a life led far from the fogs of Baker Street. He seemed to bring a whiff of his strong, fresh, bracing, east-coast air with him as he entered. Having shaken hands with each of us, he was about to sit down, when, his eye rested upon the paper with the curious markings, which I had just examined and left upon the table.

'Well, Mr Holmes, what do you make of these?' he cried. 'They told me that you were fond of queer mysteries, and

I don't think you can find a queerer one than that. I sent the paper on ahead, so that you might have time to study it before I came.'

'It is certainly rather a curious production,' said Holmes. 'At first sight it would appear to be some childish prank. It consists of a number of absurd little figures dancing across the paper upon which they are drawn. Why should you attribute any importance to so grotesque an object?'

'I never should, Mr Holmes. But my wife does. It is frightening her to death. She says nothing, but I can see terror in her eyes. Th at's why I want to sift the matter to the bottom.'

Holmes held up the paper so that the sunlight shone full upon it. It was a page torn from a notebook. Th e markings were done in pencil, and ran in this way:

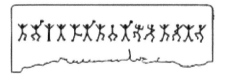

Holmes examined it for some time, and then, folding it carefully up, he placed it in his pocket-book.

'Th is promises to be a most interesting and unusual case,' said he. 'You gave me a few particulars in your letter, Mr Hilton Cubitt, but I should be very much obliged if you would kindly go over it all again for the benefit of my friend, Dr Watson.'

'I'm not much of a storyteller,' said our visitor, nervously clasping and unclasping his great, strong hands. 'You'll just ask me anything that I don't make clear. I'll begin at the time of my marriage last year, but I want to say first of all that, though I'm not a rich man, my people have been at Riding Thorpe for a matter of five centuries, and there is no better-known family in the County of Norfolk. Last year I came up to London for the Jubilee, and I stopped at a boarding-house in Russell Square, because Parker, the vicar of our parish, was staying in it. There was an American young lady there—Patrick was the name—Elsie Patrick. In some way we became friends, until before my month was up I was as much in love as man could be. We were quietly married at a registry office, and we returned to Norfolk a wedded couple. You'll think it very mad, Mr Holmes, that a man of a good old family should marry a wife in this fashion, knowing nothing of her past or of her people, but if you saw her and knew her, it would help you to understand.

'She was very straight about it, was Elsie. I can't say that she did not give me every chance of getting out of it if I wished to do so. "I have had some very disagreeable associations in my life," said she, "I wish to forget all about them. I would rather never allude to the past, for it is very painful to me. If you take me, Hilton, you will take a woman who has nothing that she need be personally ashamed of; but you will have to be content with my word for it, and to allow me to be silent as to all that passed up to the time when I became yours. If these conditions are too hard, then go back to Norfolk, and leave me to the lonely life in which you found me." It was only the day before our wedding that she said those very words to me. I told her that I was content to take her on her own terms, and I have been as good as my word.

'Well, we have been married now for a year, and very happy we have been. But about a month ago, at the end of June, I saw for the first time signs of trouble. One day my wife received a letter from America. I saw the American stamp. She turned deadly white, read the letter, and threw it into the fire. She made no allusion to it afterwards, and I made none, for a promise is a promise, but she has never known an easy hour from that moment. There is always a look of fear upon her face—a look as if she were waiting and expecting. She would do better to trust me. She would find that I was her best friend. But until she speaks, I can say nothing. Mind you, she is a truthful woman, Mr Holmes, and whatever trouble there may have been in her past life it has been no fault of hers. I am only a simple Norfolk squire, but there is not a man in England who ranks his family honour more highly than I do. She knows it well, and she knew it well before she married me. She would never bring any stain upon it—of that I am sure.

'Well, now I come to the queer part of my story. About a week ago—it was the Tuesday of last week—I found on one of the window-sills a number of absurd little dancing figures like these upon the paper. They were scrawled with chalk. I thought that it was the stable-boy who had drawn them, but the lad swore he knew nothing about it. Anyhow, they had come there during the night. I had them washed out, and I only mentioned the matter to my wife afterwards.

To my surprise, she took it very seriously, and begged me if any more came to let her see them. None did come for a week, and then yesterday morning I found this paper lying on the sundial in the garden. I showed it to Elsie, and down she dropped in a dead faint. Since then she has looked like a woman in a dream, half dazed, and with terror always lurking in her eyes. It was then that I wrote and sent the paper to you, Mr Holmes. It was not a thing that I could take to the police, for they would have laughed at me, but you will tell me what to do. I am not a rich man, but if there is any danger threatening my little woman, I would spend my last copper to shield her.'

He was a fine creature, this man of the old English soil— simple, straight, and gentle, with his great, earnest blue eyes and broad, comely face. His love for his wife and his trust in her shone in his features. Holmes had listened to his story with the utmost attention, and now he sat for some time in silent thought.

'Don't you think, Mr Cubitt,' said he, at last, 'that your best plan would be to make a direct appeal to your wife, and to ask her to share her secret with you?'

Hilton Cubitt shook his massive head.

'A promise is a promise, Mr Holmes. If Elsie wished to tell me she would. If not, it is not for me to force her confidence. But I am justified in taking my own line—and I will.'

'Then I will help you with all my heart. In the first place, have you heard of any strangers being seen in your neighbourhood?'

'No.'

'I presume that it is a very quiet place. Any fresh face would cause comment?'

'In the immediate neighbourhood, yes. But we have several small watering-places not very far away. And the farmers take in lodgers.'

'These hieroglyphics have evidently a meaning. If it is a purely arbitrary one, it may be impossible for us to solve it. If, on the other hand, it is systematic, I have no doubt that we shall get to the bottom of it. But this particular sample is so short that I can do nothing, and the facts which you have brought me are so indefinite that we have no basis for an investigation. I would suggest that you return to Norfolk, that you keep a keen look-out, and that you take an exact copy of any fresh dancing men which may appear. It is a thousand pities that we have not a reproduction of those which were done in chalk upon the window-sill. Make a discreet inquiry also as to any strangers in the neighbourhood. When you have collected some fresh evidence, come to me again. That is the best advice which I can give you, Mr Hilton Cubitt. If there are any pressing fresh developments, I shall be always ready to run down and see you in your Norfolk home.'

The interview left Sherlock Holmes very thoughtful, and several times in the next few days I saw him take his slip of paper from his notebook and look long and earnestly at the curious figures inscribed upon it. He made no allusion to the affair, however, until one afternoon a fortnight or so later. I was going out when he called me back.

'You had better stay here, Watson.'

'Why?'

'Because I had a wire from Hilton Cubitt this morning. You remember Hilton Cubitt, of the dancing men? He was to reach Liverpool Street at one-twenty. He may be here at any moment. I gather from his wire that there have been some new incidents of importance.'

We had not long to wait, for our Norfolk squire came straight from the station as fast as a hansom could bring him. He was looking worried and depressed, with tired eyes and a lined forehead.

'It's getting on my nerves, this business, Mr Holmes,' said he, as he sank, like a wearied man, into an armchair. 'It's bad enough to feel that you are surrounded by unseen, unknown folk, who have some kind of design upon you, but when, in addition to that, you know that it is just killing your wife by inches, then it becomes as much as flesh and blood can endure. She's wearing away under it just wearing away before my eyes.'

'Has she said anything yet?'

'No, Mr Holmes, she has not. And yet there have been times when the poor girl has wanted to speak, and yet could not quite bring herself to take the plunge. I have tried to help her, but I dare say I did it clumsily, and scared her from it. She has spoken about my old family, and our reputation in the county, and our pride in our unsullied honour, and I always felt it was leading to the point, but somehow it turned off before we got there.'

'But you have found out something for yourself?'

'A good deal, Mr Holmes. I have several fresh dancing-men pictures for you to examine, and, what is more important, I have seen the fellow.'

'What, the man who draws them?'

'Yes, I saw him at his work. But I will tell you everything in order. When I got back after my visit to you, the very first thing I saw next morning was a fresh crop of dancing men. Th ey had been drawn in chalk upon the black wooden door of the tool-house, which stands beside the lawn in full view of the front windows. I took an exact copy, and here it is.'

He unfolded a paper and laid it upon the table. Here is a copy of the hieroglyphics:

'Excellent!' said Holmes. 'Excellent! Pray continue.'

'When I had taken the copy, I rubbed out the marks, but, two mornings later, a fresh inscription had appeared. I have a copy of it here':

Holmes rubbed his hands and chuckled with delight.

'Our material is rapidly accumulating,' said he.

'Th ree days later a message was left scrawled upon paper, and placed under a pebble upon the sundial. Here it is. Th e characters are, as you see, exactly the same as the last one. After that I determined to lie in wait, so I got out my revolver and I sat up in my study, which overlooks the lawn and garden. About two in the morning I was seated by the window, all being dark save for the moonlight outside, when I heard steps behind me, and there was my wife in her dressing-gown. She implored me to come to bed. I told her frankly that I wished to see who it was who played such absurd tricks upon us. She answered that it was some senseless practical joke, and that I should not take any notice of it.

'"If it really annoys you, Hilton, we might go and travel, you and I, and so avoid this nuisance."

'"What, be driven out of our own house by a practical joker?" said I. "Why, we should have the whole county laughing at us."

'"Well, come to bed," said she, "and we can discuss it in the morning."

'Suddenly, as she spoke, I saw her white face grow whiter yet in the moonlight, and her hand tightened upon my shoulder. Something was moving in the shadow of the tool-house. I saw a dark, creeping figure which crawled round the corner and squatted in front of the door. Seizing my pistol, I was rushing out, when my wife threw her arms round me and held me with convulsive strength. I tried to throw her off, but she clung to me most desperately. At last I got clear, but by the time I had opened the door and reached the house the creature was gone. He had left a trace of his presence, however, for there on the door was the very same arrangement of dancing men which had already twice appeared, and which I have copied on that paper. There was no other sign of the fellow anywhere, though I ran all over the grounds. And yet the amazing thing is that he must have been there all the time, for when I examined the door again in the morning he had scrawled some more of his pictures under the line which I had already seen.'

'Have you that fresh drawing?'

'Yes, it is very short, but I made a copy of it, and here it is.' Again he produced a paper. The new dance was in this form:

'Tell me,' said Holmes—and I could see by his eyes that he was much excited—'was this a mere addition to the first, or did it appear to be entirely separate?'

'It was on a different panel of the door.'

'Excellent! This is far the most important of all for our purpose. It fills me with hopes. Now, Mr Hilton Cubitt, please continue your most interesting statement.'

'I have nothing more to say, Mr Holmes, except that I was angry with my wife that night for having held me back when I might have caught the skulking rascal. She said that she feared that I might come to harm. For an instant it had crossed my mind that perhaps what she really feared was that he might come to harm, for I could not doubt that she knew who this man was, and what he meant by these strange signals. But there is a tone in my wife's voice, Mr

Holmes, and a look in her eyes which forbid doubt, and I am sure that it was indeed my own safety that was in her mind. There's the whole case, and now I want your advice as to what I ought to do. My own inclination is to put half a dozen of my farm lads in the shrubbery, and when this fellow comes again to give him such a hiding that he will leave us in peace for the future.'

'I fear it is too deep a case for such simple remedies,' said Holmes. 'How long can you stay in London?'

'I must go back to-day. I would not leave my wife alone at night for anything. She is very nervous, and begged me to come back.'

'I dare say you are right. But if you could have stopped, I might possibly have been able to return with you in a day or two. Meanwhile you will leave me these papers, and I think that it is very likely that I shall be able to pay you a visit shortly and to throw some light upon your case.'

Sherlock Holmes preserved his calm professional manner until our visitor had left us, although it was easy for me, who knew him so well, to see that he was profoundly excited. The moment that Hilton Cubitt's broad back had disappeared through the door my comrade rushed to the table, laid out all the slips of paper containing dancing men in front of him, and threw himself into an intricate and elaborate calculation. For two hours I watched him as he covered sheet after sheet of paper with figures and letters, so completely absorbed in his task that he had evidently forgotten my presence. Sometimes he was making progress and whistled and sang at his work; sometimes he was puzzled, and would sit for long spells with a furrowed brow and a vacant eye. Finally he sprang from his chair with a cry of satisfaction, and walked up and down the room rubbing his hands together. Th en he wrote a long telegram upon a cable form. 'If my answer to this is as I hope, you will have a very pretty case to add to your collection, Watson,' said he. 'I expect that we shall be able to go down to Norfolk to-morrow, and to take our friend some very definite news as to the secret of his annoyance.'

I confess that I was filled with curiosity, but I was aware that Holmes liked to make his disclosures at his own time and in his own way, so I waited until it should suit him to take me into his confidence.

But there was a delay in that answering telegram, and two days of impatience followed, during which Holmes pricked up his ears at every ring of the bell. On the evening of the second there came a letter from Hilton Cubitt. All was quiet with him, save that a long inscription had appeared that morning upon the pedestal of the sundial. He inclosed a copy of it, which is here reproduced:

Holmes bent over this grotesque frieze for some minutes, and then suddenly sprang to his feet with an exclamation of surprise and dismay. His face was haggard with anxiety.

'We have let this affair go far enough,' said he. 'Is there a train to North Walsham to-night?'

I turned up the time-table. The last had just gone.

'Then we shall breakfast early and take the very first in the morning,' said Holmes. 'Our presence is most urgently needed. Ah! here is our expected cablegram. One moment, Mrs Hudson, there may be an answer. No, that is quite as I expected. This message makes it even more essential that we should not lose an hour in letting Hilton Cubitt know how matters stand, for it is a singular and a dangerous web in which our simple Norfolk squire is entangled.'

So, indeed, it proved, and as I come to the dark conclusion of a story which had seemed to me to be only childish and bizarre, I experience once again the dismay and horror with which I was filled. Would that I had some brighter ending to communicate to my readers, but these are the chronicles of fact, and I must follow to their dark crisis the strange chain of events which for some days made Riding Thorpe Manor a household word through the length and breadth of England.

We had hardly alighted at North Walsham, and mentioned the name of our destination, when the station-master hurried towards us. 'I suppose that you are the detectives from London?' said he.

A look of annoyance passed over Holmes' face.

'What makes you think such a thing?'

'Because Inspector Martin from Norwich has just passed through. But maybe you are the surgeons. She's not dead—

or wasn't by last accounts. You may be in time to save her yet—though it be for the gallows.'

Holmes' brow was dark with anxiety.

'We are going to Riding Thorpe Manor,' said he, 'but we have heard nothing of what has passed there.'

'It's a terrible business,' said the station-master. 'They are shot, both Mr Hilton Cubitt and his wife. She shot him and then herself—so the servants say. He's dead and her life is despaired of. Dear, dear, one of the oldest families in the County of Norfolk, and one of the most honoured.'

Without a word Holmes hurried to a carriage, and during the long seven-mile drive he never opened his mouth. Seldom have I seen him so utterly despondent. He had been uneasy during all our journey from town, and I had observed that he had turned over the morning papers with anxious attention, but now this sudden realization of his worst fears left him in a blank melancholy. He leaned back in his seat, lost in gloomy speculation. Yet there was much around to interest us, for we were passing through as singular a country-side as any in England, where a few scattered cottages represented the population of to-day, while on every hand enormous square-towered churches bristled up from the flat, green landscape and told of the glory and prosperity of old East Anglia. At last the violet rim of the German Ocean appeared over the green edge of the Norfolk coast, and the driver pointed with his whip to two old brick and timber gables which projected from a grove of trees. 'That's Riding Thorpe Manor,' said he.

As we drove up to the porticoed front door, I observed in front of it, beside the tennis lawn, the black tool-house and the pedestalled sundial with which we had such strange associations. A dapper little man, with a quick, alert manner and a waxed moustache, had just descended from a high dog-cart. He introduced himself as Inspector Martin, of the Norfolk Constabulary, and he was considerably astonished when he heard the name of my companion.

'Why, Mr Holmes, the crime was only committed at three this morning. How could you hear of it in London and get to the spot as soon as I?'

'I anticipated it. I came in the hope of preventing it.'

'Then you must have important evidence, of which we are ignorant, for they were said to be a most united couple.'

'I have only the evidence of the dancing men,' said Holmes. 'I will explain the matter to you later. Meanwhile, since it is too late to prevent this tragedy, I am very anxious that I should use the knowledge which I possess in order to insure that justice be done. Will you associate me in your investigation, or will you prefer that I should act independently?'

'I should be proud to feel that we were acting together, Mr Holmes,' said the inspector, earnestly.

'In that case I should be glad to hear the evidence and to examine the premises without an instant of unnecessary delay.'

Inspector Martin had the good sense to allow my friend to do things in his own fashion, and contented himself with carefully noting the results. The local surgeon, an old, white-haired man, had just come down from Mrs Hilton Cubitt's room, and he reported that her injuries were serious, but not necessarily fatal. The bullet had passed through the front of her brain, and it would probably be some time before she could regain consciousness. On the question of whether she had been shot or had shot herself, he would not venture to express any decided opinion. Certainly the bullet had been discharged at very close quarters. There was only the one pistol found in the room, two barrels of which had been emptied. Mr Hilton Cubitt had been shot through the heart. It was equally conceivable that he had shot her and then himself, or that she had been the criminal, for the revolver lay upon the floor midway between them.

'Has he been moved?' asked Holmes.

'We have moved nothing except the lady. We could not leave her lying wounded upon the floor.'

'How long have you been here, doctor?'

'Since four o'clock.'

'Anyone else?'

'Yes, the constable here.'

'And you have touched nothing?'

'Nothing.'

'You have acted with great discretion. Who sent for you?'

'The housemaid, Saunders.'

'Was it she who gave the alarm?'

'She and Mrs King, the cook.'

'Where are they now?'

'In the kitchen, I believe.'

'Then I think we had better hear their story at once.'

The old hall, oak-panelled and high-windowed, had been turned into a court of investigation. Holmes sat in a great, old-fashioned chair, his inexorable eyes gleaming out of his haggard face. I could read in them a set purpose to devote his life to this quest until the client whom he had failed to save should at last be avenged. The trim Inspector Martin, the old, grey-headed country doctor, myself, and a stolid village policeman made up the rest of that strange company.

The two women told their story clearly enough. They had been aroused from their sleep by the sound of an explosion, which had been followed a minute later by a second one. They slept in adjoining rooms, and Mrs King had rushed in to Saunders. Together they had descended the stairs. The door of the study was open, and a candle was burning upon the table. Their master lay upon his face in the centre of the room. He was quite dead. Near the window his wife was crouching, her head leaning against the wall. She was horribly wounded, and the side of her face was red with blood. She breathed heavily, but was incapable of saying anything. The passage, as well as the room, was full of smoke and the smell of powder. The window was certainly shut and fastened upon the inside. Both women were positive upon the point. They had at once sent for the doctor and for the constable. Then, with the aid of the groom and the stable-boy, they had conveyed their injured mistress to her room. Both she and her husband had occupied the bed.

She was clad in her dress—he in his dressing gown, over his night-clothes. Nothing had been moved in the study. So far as they knew, there had never been any quarrel between husband and wife. They had always looked upon them as a very united couple.

These were the main points of the servants' evidence. In answer to Inspector Martin, they were clear that every door was fastened upon the inside, and that no one could have escaped from the house. In answer to Holmes, they both remembered that they were conscious of the smell of powder from the moment that they ran out of their rooms upon the top floor. 'I commend that fact very carefully to your attention,' said Holmes to his professional colleague. 'And now I think that we are in a position to undertake a thorough examination of the room.'

The study proved to be a small chamber, lined on three sides with books, and with a writing-table facing an ordinary window, which looked out upon the garden. Our first attention was given to the body of the unfortunate squire, whose huge frame lay stretched across the room. His disordered dress showed that he had been hastily aroused from sleep. The bullet had been fired at him from the front, and had remained in his body after penetrating the heart. His death had certainly been instantaneous and painless. There was no powder-marking either upon his dressing-gown or on his hands. According to the country surgeon, the lady had stains upon her face, but none upon her hand.

'The absence of the latter means nothing, though its

presence may mean everything,' said Holmes. 'Unless the powder from a badly fitting cartridge happens to spurt backwards, one may fire many shots without leaving a sign. I would suggest that Mr Cubitt's body may now be removed. I suppose, Doctor, you have not recovered the bullet which wounded the lady?'

'A serious operation will be necessary before that can be done. But there are still four cartridges in the revolver. Two have been fired and two wounds inflicted, so that each bullet can be accounted for.'

'So it would seem,' said Holmes. 'Perhaps you can account also for the bullet which has so obviously struck the edge of the window?'

He had turned suddenly, and his long, thin finger was pointing to a hole which had been drilled right through the lower window-sash, about an inch above the bottom.

'By George!' cried the inspector. 'How ever did you see that?'

'Because I looked for it.'

'Wonderful!' said the country doctor. 'You are certainly right, sir. Then a third shot has been fired, and therefore a third person must have been present. But who could that have been, and how could he have got away?'

'That is the problem which we are now about to solve,' said Sherlock Holmes. 'You remember, Inspector Martin, when the servants said that on leaving their room they were at once conscious of a smell of powder, I remarked that the point was an extremely important one?'

'Yes, sir; but I confess I did not quite follow you.'

'It suggested that at the time of the firing, the window as well as the door of the room had been open. Otherwise the fumes of powder could not have been blown so rapidly through the house. A draught in the room was necessary for that. Both door and window were only open for a very short time, however.'

'How do you prove that?'

'Because the candle was not guttered.'

'Capital!' cried the inspector. 'Capital!'

'Feeling sure that the window had been open at the time of the tragedy, I conceived that there might have been a third person in the affair, who stood outside this opening and fired through it. Any shot directed at this person might hit the sash. I looked, and there, sure enough, was the bullet mark!'

'But how came the window to be shut and fastened?'

'The woman's first instinct would be to shut and fasten the window. But, halloa! what is this?'

It was a lady's handbag which stood upon the study table—a trim little handbag of crocodile-skin and silver. Holmes opened it and turned the contents out. There were twenty fifty-pound notes of the Bank of England, held together by an india-rubber band—nothing else.

'This must be preserved, for it will figure in the trial,' said Holmes, as he handed the bag with its contents to the inspector. 'It is now necessary that we should try to throw some light upon this third bullet, which has clearly, from the splintering of the wood, been fired from inside the room. I should like to see Mrs King, the cook, again. You said, Mrs King, that you were awakened by a *loud* explosion. When you said that, did you mean that it seemed to you to be louder than the second one?'

'Well, sir, it wakened me from my sleep, and so it is hard to judge. But it did seem very loud.'

'You don't think that it might have been two shots fired almost at the same instant?'

'I am sure I couldn't say, sir.'

'I believe that it was undoubtedly so. I rather think, Inspector Martin, that we have now exhausted all that this room can teach us. If you will kindly step round with me, we shall see what fresh evidence the garden has to offer.'

A flower-bed extended up to the study window, and we all broke into an exclamation as we approached it. The flowers were trampled down, and the soft soil was imprinted all over with footmarks. Large, masculine feet they were, with peculiarly long, sharp toes. Holmes hunted about among the grass and leaves like a retriever after a wounded bird. Then, with a cry of satisfaction, he bent forward and picked up a little brazen cylinder.

'I thought so,' said he, 'the revolver had an ejector, and here is the third cartridge. I really think, Inspector Martin, that our case is almost complete.'

The country inspector's face had shown his intense amazement at the rapid and masterful progress of Holmes' investigation. At first he had shown some disposition to assert his own position, but now he was overcome with admiration, and ready to follow without question wherever Holmes led.

'Whom do you suspect?' he asked.

'I'll go into that later. There are several points in this problem which I have not been able to explain to you yet. Now that I have got so far, I had best proceed on my own lines, and then clear the whole matter up once and for all.'

'Just as you wish, Mr Holmes, so long as we get our man.'

'I have no desire to make mysteries, but it is impossible at the moment of action to enter into long and complex explanations. I have the threads of this affair all in my hand. Even if this lady should never recover consciousness, we can still reconstruct the events of last night, and insure that justice be done. First of all, I wish to know whether there is any inn in this neighbourhood known as "Elrige's"?'

The servants were cross-questioned, but none of them had heard of such a place. The stable-boy threw a light upon the matter by remembering that a farmer of that name lived some miles off, in the direction of East Ruston.

'Is it a lonely farm?'

'Very lonely, sir.'

'Perhaps they have not heard yet of all that happened here during the night?'

'Maybe not, sir.'

Holmes thought for a little, and then a curious smile played over his face.

'Saddle a horse, my lad,' said he. 'I shall wish you to take a note to Elrige's Farm.'

He took from his pocket the various slips of the dancing men. With these in front of him, he worked for some time at the study-table. Finally he handed a note to the boy, with directions to put it into the hands of the person to whom it was addressed, and especially to answer no questions of any sort which might be put to him. I saw the outside of the note, addressed in straggling, irregular characters, very unlike Holmes' usual precise hand. It was consigned to Mr Abe Slaney, Elrige's Farm, East Ruston, Norfolk.

'I think, Inspector,' Holmes remarked, 'that you would do well to telegraph for an escort, as, if my calculations prove to be correct, you may have a particularly dangerous prisoner to convey to the county gaol. The boy who takes this note could no doubt forward your telegram. If there is an afternoon train to town, Watson, I think we should do well to take it, as I have a chemical analysis of some interest to finish, and this investigation draws rapidly to a close.'

When the youth had been dispatched with the note, Sherlock Holmes gave his instructions to the servants. If any visitor were to call asking for Mrs Hilton Cubitt, no information should be given as to her condition, but he was to be shown at once into the drawing-room. He impressed these points upon them with the utmost earnestness. Finally he led the way into the drawing-room, with the remark that the business was now out of our hands, and that we must while away the time as best we might until we could see what was in store for us. The doctor had departed to his patients, and only the inspector and myself remained.

'I think that I can help you to pass an hour in an interesting and profitable manner,' said Holmes, drawing his chair up to the table, and spreading out in front of him the various papers upon which were recorded the antics of the dancing men. 'As to you, friend Watson, I owe you every atonement for having allowed your natural curiosity to remain so long unsatisfied. To you, Inspector, the whole incident may appeal as a remarkable professional study. I must tell you, first of all, the interesting circumstances connected with the previous consultations which Mr Hilton Cubitt has had with me in Baker Street.' He then shortly recapitulated the facts which have already been recorded. 'I have here in front of me these singular productions, at which one might smile, had they not proved themselves to be the forerunners of so terrible a tragedy. I am fairly familiar with all forms of secret writings, and am myself the author of a trifling monograph upon the subject, in which I analyze one hundred and sixty separate ciphers, but I confess that this is entirely new to me. Th e object of those who invented the system has apparently been to conceal that these characters convey a message, and to give the idea that they are the mere random sketches of children.

'Having once recognized, however, that the symbols stood for letters, and having applied the rules which guide us in all forms of secret writings, the solution was easy enough. Th e first message submitted to me was so short that it was impossible for me to do more than to say, with some confidence, that the symbol stood for E. As you are aware, E is the most common letter in the English alphabet, and it predominates to so marked an extent that even in a short sentence one would expect to find it most often. Out of fifteen symbols in the first message, four were the same, so it was reasonable to set this down as E. It is true that in some cases the figure was bearing a flag, and in some cases not, but it was probable, from the way in which the flags were distributed, that they were used to break the sentence up into words. I accepted this as a hypothesis, and noted that E was represented by X

'But now came the real diffi culty of the inquiry. Th e order of the English letters after E is by no means well marked, and any preponderance which may be shown in an average of a printed sheet may be reversed in a single short sentence. Speaking roughly, T, A, O, I, N, S, H, R, D, and L are the numerical order in which letters occur; but T, A, O, and I are very nearly abreast of each other, and it would be an endless task to try each combination until a meaning was arrived at. I therefore waited for fresh material. In my second interview with Mr Hilton Cubitt he was able to give me two other short sentences and one message, which appeared—since there was no flag—to be a single word. Here are the symbols. Now, in the single word I have already got the two E's coming second and fourth in a word of five letters. It might be 'sever,' or 'lever,' or 'never.' Th ere can be no question that the latter as a reply to an appeal is far the most probable, and the circumstances pointed to its being a reply written by the lady. Accepting it as correct, we are now able to say that the symbols stand respectively for N, V, and R.

'Even now I was in considerable diffi culty, but a happy thought put me in possession of several other letters. It occurred to me that if these appeals came, as I expected, from someone who had been intimate with the lady in her early life, a combination which contained two E's with three letters between might very well stand for the name 'ELSIE.' On examination I found that such a combination formed the termination of the message which was three times repeated. It was certainly some appeal to 'Elsie.' In this way I had got my L, S, and I. But what appeal could it be? Th ere were only four letters in the word which preceded 'Elsie,' and it ended in E. Surely the word must be 'COME.' I tried all other four letters ending in E, but could find none to fit the case. So now I was in possession of C, O, and M, and I was in a position to attack the first message once more, dividing it into words and putting dots for each symbol which was still unknown. So treated, it worked out in this fashion:

.M .ERE ..E SL.NE.

'Now the first letter can only be A, which is a most useful discovery, since it occurs no fewer than three times in this short sentence, and the H is also apparent in the second word. Now it becomes:

AM HERE A.E SLANE.

Or, filling in the obvious vacancies in the name:

AM HERE ABE SLANEY.

I had so many letters now that I could proceed with considerable confidence to the second message, which worked out in this fashion:

A. ELRI.ES.

Here I could only make sense by putting T and G for the missing letters, and supposing that the name was that of some house or inn at which the writer was staying.'

Inspector Martin and I had listened with the utmost interest to the full and clear account of how my friend had produced results which had led to so complete a command over our difficulties.

'What did you do then, sir?' asked the inspector.

'I had every reason to suppose that this Abe Slaney was an American, since Abe is an American contraction, and since a letter from America had been the starting-point of all the trouble. I had also every cause to think that there was some criminal secret in the matter. The lady's allusions to her past, and her refusal to take her husband into her confidence, both pointed in that direction. I therefore cabled to my friend, Wilson Hargreave, of the New York Police Bureau, who has more than once made use of my knowledge of London crime. I asked him whether the name of Abe Slaney was known to him. Here is his reply: 'The most dangerous crook in Chicago.' On the very evening upon which I had his answer, Hilton Cubitt sent me the last message from Slaney. Working with known letters, it took this form:

ELSIE .RE.ARE TO MEET THY GO.

The addition of a P and a D completed a message which showed me that the rascal was proceeding from persuasion to threats, and my knowledge of the crooks of Chicago prepared me to find that he might very rapidly put his words into action. I at once came to Norfolk with my friend and colleague, Dr Watson, but, unhappily, only in time to find that the worst had already occurred.'

'It is a privilege to be associated with you in the handling of a case,' said the inspector, warmly. 'You will excuse me, however, if I speak frankly to you. You are only answerable to yourself, but I have to answer to my superiors. If this Abe Slaney, living at Elrige's, is indeed the murderer, and if he has made his escape while I am seated here, I should certainly get into serious trouble.'

'You need not be uneasy. He will not try to escape.'

'How do you know?'

'To fly would be a confession of guilt.'

'Then let us go to arrest him.'

'I expect him here every instant.'

'But why should he come?'

'Because I have written and asked him.'

'But this is incredible, Mr Holmes! Why should he come

because you have asked him? Would not such a request rather rouse his suspicions and cause him to fly?'

'I think I have known how to frame the letter,' said Sherlock Holmes. 'In fact, if I am not very much mistaken, here is the gentleman himself coming up the drive.'

A man was striding up the path which led to the door. He was a tall, handsome, swarthy fellow, clad in a suit of grey flannel, with a Panama hat, a bristling black beard, and a great, aggressive hooked nose, and flourishing a cane as he walked. He swaggered up the path as if the place belonged to him, and we heard his loud, confident peal at the bell.

'I think, gentlemen,' said Holmes, quietly, 'that we had best take up our position behind the door. Every precaution is necessary when dealing with such a fellow. You will need your handcuffs, Inspector. You can leave the talking to me.'

We waited in silence for a minute—one of those minutes which one can never forget. Then the door opened and the man stepped in. In an instant Holmes clapped a pistol to his head, and Martin slipped the handcuffs over his wrists. It was all done so swiftly and deftly that the fellow was helpless before he knew that he was attacked. He glared from one to the other of us with a pair of blazing black eyes. Then he burst into a bitter laugh.

'Well, gentlemen, you have the drop on me this time. I seem to have knocked up against something hard. But I came here in answer to a letter from Mrs Hilton Cubitt. Don't tell me that she is in this? Don't tell me that she helped to set a trap for me?'

'Mrs Hilton Cubitt was seriously injured, and is at death's door.'

The man gave a hoarse cry of grief, which rang through the house.

'You're crazy!' he cried, fiercely. 'It was he that was hurt, not she. Who would have hurt little Elsie? I may have threatened her—God forgive me!—but I would not have touched a hair of her pretty head. Take it back—you! Say that she is not hurt!'

'She was found, badly wounded, by the side of her dead husband.'

He sank with a deep groan on to the settee, and buried his face in his manacled hands. For five minutes he was silent. Then he raised his face once more, and spoke with the cold composure of despair.

'I have nothing to hide from you, gentlemen,' said he. 'If I shot the man he had his shot at me, and there's no murder in that. But if you think I could have hurt that woman, then you don't know either me or her. I tell you, there was never a man in this world loved a woman more than I loved her. I had a right to her. She was pledged to me years ago. Who was this Englishman that he should come between us? I tell you that I had the first right to her, and that I was only claiming my own.'

'She broke away from your influence when she found the man that you are,' said Holmes, sternly. 'She fled from America to avoid you, and she married an honourable gentleman in England. You dogged her and followed her and made her life a misery to her, in order to induce her to abandon the husband whom she loved and respected in order to fly with you, whom she feared and hated. You have ended by bringing about the death of a noble man and driving his wife to suicide. That is your record in this business, Mr Abe Slaney, and you will answer for it to the law.'

'If Elsie dies, I care nothing what becomes of me,' said the American. He opened one of his hands, and looked at a note crumpled up in his palm. 'See here, mister,' he cried, with a gleam of suspicion in his eyes, 'you're not trying to scare me over this, are you? If the lady is hurt as bad as you say, who was it that wrote this note?' He tossed it forwards on to the table.

'I wrote it, to bring you here.'

'You wrote it? There was no one on earth outside the Joint who knew the secret of the dancing men. How came you to write it?'

'What one man can invent another can discover,' said Holmes. 'There is a cab coming to convey you to Norwich, Mr Slaney. But, meanwhile, you have time to make some small reparation for the injury you have wrought. Are you aware that Mrs Hilton Cubitt has herself lain under grave suspicion of the murder of her husband, and that it was only my presence here, and the knowledge which I happened to possess, which has saved her from the accusation? The least that you owe her is to make it clear to the whole world that she was in no way, directly or indirectly, responsible for his tragic end.'

'I ask nothing better,' said the American. 'I guess the very best case I can make for myself is the absolute naked truth.'

'It is my duty to warn you that it will be used against you,' cried the inspector, with the magnificent fair-play of the British criminal law.

Slaney shrugged his shoulders.

'I'll chance that,' said he. 'First of all, I want you gentlemen to understand that I have known this lady since she was a child. There were seven of us in a gang in Chicago, and Elsie's father was the boss of the Joint. He was a clever man, was old Patrick. It was he who invented that writing, which would pass as a child's scrawl unless you just happened to have the key to it. Well, Elsie learned some of our ways, but she couldn't stand the business, and she had a bit of honest money of her own, so she gave us all the slip and got away to London. She had been engaged to me, and she would have married me, I believe, if I had taken over another profession, but she would have nothing to do with anything on the cross. It was only after her marriage to this Englishman that I was able to find out where she was. I wrote to her, but got no answer. After that I came over, and, as letters were no use, I put my messages where she could read them.

'Well, I have been here a month now. I lived in that farm, where I had a room down below, and could get in and out every night, and no one the wiser. I tried all I could to coax Elsie away. I knew that she read the messages, for once she wrote an answer under one of them. Then my temper got the better of me, and I began to threaten her. She sent me a letter then, imploring me to go away, and saying that it would break her heart if any scandal should come upon her husband. She said that she would come down when her husband was asleep at three in the morning, and speak with me through the end window, if I would go away afterwards and leave her in peace. She came down and brought money with her, trying to bribe me to go. This made me mad, and I caught her arm and tried to pull her through the window. At that moment in rushed the husband with his revolver in his hand. Elsie had sunk down upon the floor, and we were face to face. I was heeled also, and I held up my gun to scare him off and let me get away. He fired and missed me. I pulled off almost at the same instant, and down he dropped. I made away across the garden, and as I went I heard the window shut behind me. That's God's truth, gentlemen, every word of it; and I heard no more about it until that lad came riding up with a note which made me walk in here, like a jay, and give myself into your hands.'

A cab had driven up whilst the American had been talking. Two uniformed policemen sat inside. Inspector Martin rose and touched his prisoner on the shoulder.

'It is time for us to go.'

'Can I see her first?'

'No, she is not conscious. Mr Sherlock Holmes, I only hope that, if ever again I have an important case, I shall have the good fortune to have you by my side.'

We stood at the window and watched the cab drive away. As I turned back, my eye caught the pellet of paper which the prisoner had tossed upon the table. It was the note with which Holmes had decoyed him.

'See if you can read it, Watson,' said he, with a smile.

It contained no word, but this little line of dancing men:

𖼴𖼱𖼣𖼵𖼲𖼸𖼶𖼵𖼼𖼲𖼱𖼣𖼣𖼵

'If you use the code which I have explained,' said Holmes, 'you will find that it simply means "Come here at once." I was convinced that it was an invitation which he would not refuse, since he could never imagine that it could come from anyone but the lady. And so, my dear Watson, we have ended by turning the dancing men to good when they have so often been the agents of evil, and I think that I have fulfilled my promise of giving you something unusual for your notebook. Three-forty is our train, and I fancy we should be back in Baker Street for dinner.

Only one word of epilogue. Th e American, Abe Slaney, was condemned to death at the winter assizes at Norwich, but his penalty was changed to penal servitude in consideration of mitigating circumstances, and the certainty that Hilton Cubitt had fired the first shot. Of Mrs Hilton Cubitt I only know that I have heard she recovered entirely, and that she still remains a widow, devoting her whole life to the care of the poor and to the administration of her husband's estate.

the final problem

It is with a heavy heart that I take up my pen to write these the last words in which I shall ever record the singular gifts by which my friend Mr Sherlock Holmes was distinguished. In an incoherent and, as I deeply feel, an entirely inadequate fashion, I have endeavoured to give some account of my strange experiences in his company from the chance which first brought us together at the period of the 'Study in Scarlet,' up to the time of his interference in the matter of the 'Naval Treaty'—an interference which had the unquestionable effect of preventing a serious international complication. It was my intention to have stopped there, and to have said nothing of that event which has created a void in my life which the lapse of two years has done little to fill. My hand has been forced, however, by the recent letters in which Colonel James Moriarty defends the memory of his brother, and I have no choice but to lay the facts before the public exactly as they occurred. I alone know the absolute truth of the matter, and I am satisfied that the time has come when no good purpose is to be served by its suppression. As far as I know, there have been only three accounts in the public press: that in the *Journal de Geneve* on May 6th, 1891, the Reuter's despatch in the English papers on May 7th, and finally the recent letter to which I have alluded. Of these the first and second were extremely condensed, while the last is, as I shall now show, an absolute perversion of the facts. It lies with me to tell for the first time what really took place between Professor Moriarty and Mr Sherlock Holmes.

It may be remembered that after my marriage, and my subsequent start in private practice, the very intimate relations which had existed between Holmes and myself became to some extent modified. He still came to me from time to time when he desired a companion in his investigation, but these occasions grew more and more seldom, until I find that in the year 1890 there were only three cases of which I retain any record. During the winter of that year and the early spring of 1891, I saw in the papers that he had been engaged by the French government upon a matter of supreme importance, and I received two notes from Holmes, dated from Narbonne and from Nimes, from which I gathered that his stay in France was likely to be a long one. It was with some surprise, therefore, that I saw him walk into my consulting-room upon the evening of April 24th. It struck me that he was looking even paler and thinner than usual.

'Yes, I have been using myself up rather too freely,' he remarked, in answer to my look rather than to my words; 'I have been a little pressed of late. Have you any objection to my closing your shutters?'

The only light in the room came from the lamp upon the table at which I had been reading. Holmes edged his way round the wall and flinging the shutters together, he bolted them securely.

'You are afraid of something?' I asked.

'Well, I am.'

'Of what?'

'Of air-guns.'

'My dear Holmes, what do you mean?'

'I think that you know me well enough, Watson, to understand that I am by no means a nervous man. At the same time, it is stupidity rather than courage to refuse to recognize danger when it is close upon you. Might I trouble you for a match?' He drew in the smoke of his cigarette as if the soothing influence was grateful to him.

'I must apologize for calling so late,' said he, 'and I must further beg you to be so unconventional as to allow me to leave your house presently by scrambling over your back garden wall.'

'But what does it all mean?' I asked.

He held out his hand, and I saw in the light of the lamp that two of his knuckles were burst and bleeding.

'It is not an airy nothing, you see,' said he, smiling. 'On the contrary, it is solid enough for a man to break his hand over. Is Mrs Watson in?'

'She is away upon a visit.'

'Indeed! You are alone?'

'Quite.'

'Then it makes it the easier for me to propose that you should come away with me for a week to the Continent.'

'Where?'

'Oh, anywhere. It's all the same to me.'

There was something very strange in all this. It was not Holmes' nature to take an aimless holiday, and something about his pale, worn face told me that his nerves were at their highest tension. He saw the question in my eyes, and, putting his finger-tips together and his elbows upon his knees, he explained the situation.

'You have probably never heard of Professor Moriarty?' said he.

'Never.'

'Aye, there's the genius and the wonder of the thing!' he cried. 'The man pervades London, and no one has heard of him. That's what puts him on a pinnacle in the records of crime. I tell you, Watson, in all seriousness, that if I could beat that man, if I could free society of him, I should feel that my own career had reached its summit, and I should be prepared to turn to some more placid line in life. Between ourselves, the recent cases in which I have been of assistance to the royal family of Scandinavia, and to the French republic, have left me in such a position that I could continue to live in the quiet fashion which is most congenial to me, and to concentrate my attention upon my chemical researches. But I could not rest, Watson, I could not sit quiet in my chair, if I thought that such a man as Professor Moriarty were walking the streets of London unchallenged.'

'What has he done, then?'

'His career has been an extraordinary one. He is a man of good birth and excellent education, endowed by nature with a phenomenal mathematical faculty. At the age of twenty-one he wrote a treatise upon the Binomial Theorem, which has had a European vogue. On the strength of it he won the Mathematical Chair at one of our smaller universities, and had, to all appearances, a most brilliant career before him. But the man had hereditary tendencies of the most diabolical kind. A criminal strain ran in his blood, which, instead of being modified, was increased and rendered infinitely more dangerous by his extraordinary mental powers. Dark rumours gathered round him in the university town, and eventually he was compelled to resign his chair and to come down to London, where he set up as an army coach. So much is known to the world, but what I am telling you now is what I have myself discovered.

'As you are aware, Watson, there is no one who knows the higher criminal world of London so well as I do. For years past I have continually been conscious of some power behind the malefactor, some deep organizing power which forever stands in the way of the law, and throws its shield over the wrong-doer. Again and again in cases of the most varying sorts—forgery cases, robberies, murders—I have felt the presence of this force, and I have deduced its action in many of those undiscovered crimes in which I have not been personally consulted. For years I have endeavoured to break through the veil which shrouded it, and at last the time came when I seized my thread and followed it, until it led me, after a thousand cunning windings, to ex-Professor Moriarty of mathematical celebrity.

'He is the Napoleon of crime, Watson. He is the organizer of half that is evil and of nearly all that is undetected in this great city. He is a genius, a philosopher, an abstract thinker. He has a brain of the first order. He sits motionless, like a spider in the center of its web, but that web has a thousand radiations, and he knows well every quiver of each of them. He does little himself. He only plans. But his agents are numerous and splendidly organized. Is there a crime to be done, a paper to be abstracted, we will say, a house to be rifled, a man to be removed—the word is passed to the Professor, the matter is organized and carried out. The agent may be caught. In that case money is found for his bail or his defence. But the central power which uses the agent is never caught—never so much as suspected. This was the organization which I deduced, Watson, and which I devoted my whole energy to exposing and breaking up.

'But the Professor was fenced round with safeguards so cunningly devised that, do what I would, it seemed impossible to get evidence which would convict in a court of law. You know my powers, my dear Watson, and yet at the end of three months I was forced to confess that I had at last met an antagonist who was my intellectual equal. My horror at his crimes was lost in my admiration at his skill. But at last he made a trip—only a little, little trip—but it was more than he could afford when I was so close upon him. I had my chance, and, starting from that point, I have woven my net round him until now it is all ready to close. In three days—that is to say, on Monday next—matters will be ripe, and the Professor, with all the principal members of his gang, will be in the hands of the police. Then will come the greatest criminal trial of the century, the clearing up of over forty mysteries, and the rope for all of them; but if we move at all prematurely, you understand, they may slip out of our hands even at the last moment.

'Now, if I could have done this without the knowledge of Professor Moriarty, all would have been well. But he was too wily for that. He saw every step which I took to draw my toils round him. Again and again he strove to break away, but I as often headed him off. I tell you, my friend, that if a detailed account of that silent contest could be written, it would take its place as the most brilliant bit of thrust-and-parry work in the history of detection. Never have I risen to such a height, and never have I been so hard pressed by an opponent. He cut deep, and yet I just undercut him. This morning the last steps were taken, and three days only were wanted to complete the business. I was sitting in my room thinking the matter over, when the door opened and Professor Moriarty stood before me.

'My nerves are fairly proof, Watson, but I must confess to a start when I saw the very man who had been so much in my thoughts standing there on my threshhold. His appearance was quite familiar to me. He is extremely tall and thin, his forehead domes out in a white curve, and his two eyes are deeply sunken in his head. He is clean-shaven, pale, and ascetic-looking, retaining something of the professor in his features. His shoulders are rounded from much study, and his face protrudes forward, and is forever slowly oscillating from side to side in a curiously reptilian fashion. He peered at me with great curiosity in his puckered eyes.

"'You have less frontal development than I should have expected," said he, at last. "It is a dangerous habit to finger loaded firearms in the pocket of one's dressing-gown."

'The fact is that upon his entrance I had instantly recognized the extreme personal danger in which I lay. The only conceivable escape for him lay in silencing my tongue. In an instant I had slipped the revolver from the drawer into my pocket, and was covering him through the cloth. At his remark I drew the weapon out and laid it cocked upon the table. He still smiled and blinked, but there was something about his eyes which made me feel very glad that I had it there.

"'You evidently don't know me," said he.

"'On the contrary," I answered, "I think it is fairly evident that I do. Pray take a chair. I can spare you five minutes if you have anything to say."

"'All that I have to say has already crossed your mind," said he.

'"Then possibly my answer has crossed yours," I replied.

'"You stand fast?"

'"Absolutely."

'He clapped his hand into his pocket, and I raised the pistol from the table. But he merely drew out a memorandum-book in which he had scribbled some dates.

'"You crossed my path on the 4th of January," said he. "On the 23rd you incommoded me; by the middle of February I was seriously inconvenienced by you; at the end of March I was absolutely hampered in my plans; and now, at the close of April, I find myself placed in such a position through your continual persecution that I am in positive danger of losing my liberty. The situation is becoming an impossible one."

'"Have you any suggestion to make?" I asked.

'"You must drop it, Mr Holmes," said he, swaying his face about. "You really must, you know."

'"After Monday," said I.

'"Tut, tut," said he. "I am quite sure that a man of your intelligence will see that there can be but one outcome to this affair. It is necessary that you should withdraw. You have worked things in such a fashion that we have only one resource left. It has been an intellectual treat to me to see the way in which you have grappled with this affair, and I say, unaffectedly, that it would be a grief to me to be forced to take any extreme measure. You smile, sir, but I assure you that it really would."

'"Danger is part of my trade," I remarked.

'"That is not danger," said he. "It is inevitable destruction. You stand in the way not merely of an individual, but of a mighty organization, the full extent of which you, with all your cleverness, have been unable to realize. You must stand clear, Mr Holmes, or be trodden under foot."

'"I am afraid," said I, rising, "that in the pleasure of this conversation I am neglecting business of importance which awaits me elsewhere."

'He rose also and looked at me in silence, shaking his head sadly.

'"Well, well," said he, at last. "It seems a pity, but I have done what I could. I know every move of your game. You can do nothing before Monday. It has been a duel between you and me, Mr Holmes. You hope to place me in the dock. I tell you that I will never stand in the dock. You hope to beat me. I tell you that you will never beat me. If you are clever enough to bring destruction upon me, rest assured that I shall do as much to you."

'"You have paid me several compliments, Mr Moriarty," said I. "Let me pay you one in return when I say that if I were assured of the former eventuality I would, in the interests of the public, cheerfully accept the latter."

'"I can promise you the one, but not the other," he snarled, and so turned his rounded back upon me, and went peering and blinking out of the room.

'That was my singular interview with Professor Moriarty. I confess that it left an unpleasant effect upon my mind. His soft, precise fashion of speech leaves a conviction of sincerity which a mere bully could not produce. Of course, you will say: "Why not take police precautions against him?" the reason is that I am well convinced that it is from his agents the blow will fall. I have the best proofs that it would be so.'

'You have already been assaulted?'

'My dear Watson, Professor Moriarty is not a man who lets the grass grow under his feet. I went out about mid-day to transact some business in Oxford Street. As I passed the corner which leads from Bentinck Street on to the Welbeck Street crossing a two-horse van furiously driven whizzed round and was on me like a flash. I sprang for the footpath and saved myself by the fraction of a second. The van dashed round by Marylebone Lane and was gone in an instant. I kept to the pavement after that, Watson, but as I walked down Vere Street a brick came down from the roof of one of the houses, and was shattered to fragments at my feet. I called the police and had the place examined. There were slates and bricks piled up on the roof preparatory to some repairs, and they would have me believe that the wind had toppled over one of these. Of course I knew better, but I could prove nothing. I took a cab after that and reached my brother's rooms in Pall Mall, where I spent the day. Now I have come round to you, and on my way I was attacked by a rough with a bludgeon. I knocked him down, and the police have him in custody; but I can tell you with the most absolute confidence that no possible connection will ever be traced between the gentleman upon whose front teeth

I have barked my knuckles and the retiring mathematical coach, who is, I dare say, working out problems upon a black-board ten miles away. You will not wonder, Watson, that my first act on entering your rooms was to close your shutters, and that I have been compelled to ask your permission to leave the house by some less conspicuous exit than the front door.'

I had often admired my friend's courage, but never more than now, as he sat quietly checking off a series of incidents which must have combined to make up a day of horror.

'You will spend the night here?' I said.

'No, my friend, you might find me a dangerous guest. I have my plans laid, and all will be well. Matters have gone so far now that they can move without my help as far as the arrest goes, though my presence is necessary for a conviction. It is obvious, therefore, that I cannot do better than get away for the few days which remain before the police are at liberty to act. It would be a great pleasure to me, therefore, if you could come on to the Continent with me.'

'The practice is quiet,' said I, 'and I have an accommodating neighbour. I should be glad to come.'

'And to start to-morrow morning?'

'If necessary.'

'Oh yes, it is most necessary. Then these are your instructions, and I beg, my dear Watson, that you will obey them to the letter, for you are now playing a double-handed game with me against the cleverest rogue and the most powerful syndicate of criminals in Europe. Now listen! You will dispatch whatever luggage you intend to take by a trusty messenger unaddressed to Victoria to-night. In the morning you will send for a hansom, desiring your man to take neither the first nor the second which may present itself. Into this hansom you will jump, and you will drive to the Strand end of the Lowther Arcade, handing the address to the cabman upon a slip of paper, with a request that he will not throw it away. Have your fare ready, and the instant that your cab stops, dash through the Arcade, timing yourself to reach the other side at a quarter-past nine. You will find a small brougham waiting close to the curb, driven by a fellow with a heavy black cloak tipped at the collar with red. Into this you will step, and you will reach Victoria in time for the Continental express.'

'Where shall I meet you?'

'At the station. The second first-class carriage from the front will be reserved for us.'

'The carriage is our rendezvous, then?'

'Yes.'

It was in vain that I asked Holmes to remain for the evening. It was evident to me that he thought he might bring trouble to the roof he was under, and that that was the motive which impelled him to go. With a few hurried words as to our plans for the morrow he rose and came out with me into the garden, clambering over the wall which leads into Mortimer Street, and immediately whistling for a hansom, in which I heard him drive away.

In the morning I obeyed Holmes' injunctions to the letter. A hansom was procured with such precaution as would prevent its being one which was placed ready for us, and I drove immediately after breakfast to the Lowther Arcade, through which I hurried at the top of my speed. A brougham was waiting with a very massive driver wrapped in a dark cloak, who, the instant that I had stepped in, whipped up the horse and rattled off to Victoria Station. On my alighting there he turned the carriage, and dashed away again without so much as a look in my direction.

So far all had gone admirably. My luggage was waiting for me, and I had no difficulty in finding the carriage which Holmes had indicated, the less so as it was the only one in the train which was marked 'Engaged.' My only source of anxiety now was the non-appearance of Holmes. The station clock marked only seven minutes from the time when we were due to start. In vain I searched among the groups of travellers and leave-takers for the lithe figure of my friend. There was no sign of him. I spent a few minutes in assisting a venerable Italian priest, who was endeavouring to make a porter understand, in his broken English, that his luggage was to be booked through to Paris. Then, having taken another look round, I returned to my carriage, where I found that the porter, in spite of the ticket, had given me my decrepit Italian friend as a travelling companion. It was useless for me to explain to him that his presence was an intrusion, for my Italian was even more limited than his English, so I shrugged my shoulders resignedly, and continued to look out anxiously for my friend. A chill of fear had come over me, as I thought that his absence might mean that some blow had fallen during the night. Already the doors had all been shut and the whistle blown, when—

'My dear Watson,' said a voice, 'you have not even condescended to say good-morning.'

I turned in uncontrollable astonishment. The aged ecclesiastic had turned his face towards me. For an instant the wrinkles were smoothed away, the nose drew away from the chin, the lower lip ceased to protrude and the mouth to mumble, the dull eyes regained their fire, the drooping figure expanded. The next the whole frame collapsed again, and Holmes had gone as quickly as he had come.

'Good heavens!' I cried; 'how you startled me!'

'Every precaution is still necessary,' he whispered. 'I have reason to think that they are hot upon our trail. Ah, there is Moriarty himself.'

The train had already begun to move as Holmes spoke. Glancing back, I saw a tall man pushing his way furiously through the crowd, and waving his hand as if he desired to have the train stopped. It was too late, however, for we were rapidly gathering momentum, and an instant later had shot clear of the station.

'With all our precautions, you see that we have cut it rather fine,' said Holmes, laughing. He rose, and throwing off the black cassock and hat which had formed his disguise, he packed them away in a handbag.

'Have you seen the morning paper, Watson?'

'No.'

'You haven't seen about Baker Street, then?'

'Baker Street?'

'They set fire to our rooms last night. No great harm was done.'

'Good heavens, Holmes! this is intolerable.'

'They must have lost my track completely after their bludgeon-man was arrested. Otherwise they could not have imagined that I had returned to my rooms. They have evidently taken the precaution of watching you, however, and that is what has brought Moriarty to Victoria. You could not have made any slip in coming?'

'I did exactly what you advised.'

'Did you find your brougham?'

'Yes, it was waiting.'

'Did you recognize your coachman?'

'No.'

'It was my brother Mycroft. It is an advantage to get about in such a case without taking a mercenary into your confidence. But we must plan what we are to do about Moriarty now.'

'As this is an express, and as the boat runs in connection with it, I should think we have shaken him off very effectively.'

'My dear Watson, you evidently did not realize my meaning when I said that this man may be taken as being quite on the same intellectual plane as myself. You do not imagine that if I were the pursuer I should allow myself to be baffled by so slight an obstacle. Why, then, should you think so meanly of him?'

'What will he do?'

'What I should do?'

'What would you do, then?'

'Engage a special.'

'But it must be late.'

'By no means. This train stops at Canterbury; and there is always at least a quarter of an hour's delay at the boat. He will catch us there.'

'One would think that we were the criminals. Let us have him arrested on his arrival.'

'It would be to ruin the work of three months. We should get the big fish, but the smaller would dart right and left out of the net. On Monday we should have them all. No, an arrest is inadmissible.'

'What then?'

'We shall get out at Canterbury.'

'And then?'

'Well, then we must make a cross-country journey to Newhaven, and so over to Dieppe. Moriarty will again do what I should do. He will get on to Paris, mark down our luggage, and wait for two days at the depot. In the meantime we shall treat ourselves to a couple of carpet-bags, encourage the manufactures of the countries through which we travel, and make our way at our leisure into Switzerland, via Luxembourg and Basle.'

At Canterbury, therefore, we alighted, only to find that

we should have to wait an hour before we could get a train to Newhaven.

I was still looking rather ruefully after the rapidly disappearing luggage-van which contained my wardrobe, when Holmes pulled my sleeve and pointed up the line.

'Already, you see,' said he.

Far away, from among the Kentish woods there rose a thin spray of smoke. A minute later a carriage and engine could be seen flying along the open curve which leads to the station. We had hardly time to take our place behind a pile of luggage when it passed with a rattle and a roar, beating a blast of hot air into our faces.

'There he goes,' said Holmes, as we watched the carriage swing and rock over the points. 'There are limits, you see, to our friend's intelligence. It would have been a coup-de-maitre had he deduced what I would deduce and acted accordingly.'

'And what would he have done had he overtaken us?'

'There cannot be the least doubt that he would have made a murderous attack upon me. It is, however, a game at which two may play. The question now is whether we should take a premature lunch here, or run our chance of starving before we reach the buffet at Newhaven.'

We made our way to Brussels that night and spent two days there, moving on upon the third day as far as Strasburg. On the Monday morning Holmes had telegraphed to the London police, and in the evening we found a reply waiting for us at our hotel. Holmes tore it open, and then with a bitter curse hurled it into the grate.

'I might have known it!' he groaned. 'He has escaped!'

'Moriarty?'

'They have secured the whole gang with the exception of him. He has given them the slip. Of course, when I had left the country there was no one to cope with him. But I did think that I had put the game in their hands. I think that you had better return to England, Watson.'

'Why?'

'Because you will find me a dangerous companion now. This man's occupation is gone. He is lost if he returns to London. If I read his character right he will devote his whole energies to revenging himself upon me. He said as much in our short interview, and I fancy that he meant it. I should certainly recommend you to return to your practice.'

It was hardly an appeal to be successful with one who was an old campaigner as well as an old friend. We sat in the Strasburg salle-à-manger arguing the question for half an hour, but the same night we had resumed our journey and were well on our way to Geneva.

For a charming week we wandered up the Valley of the Rhone, and then, branching off at Leuk, we made our way over the Gemmi Pass, still deep in snow, and so, by way of Interlaken, to Meiringen. It was a lovely trip, the dainty green of the spring below, the virgin white of the winter above; but it was clear to me that never for one instant did Holmes forget the shadow which lay across him. In the homely Alpine villages or in the lonely mountain passes, I could tell by his quick glancing eyes and his sharp scrutiny of every face that passed us, that he was well convinced that, walk where we would, we could not walk ourselves clear of the danger which was dogging our footsteps.

Once, I remember, as we passed over the Gemmi, and walked along the border of the melancholy Daubensee, a large rock which had been dislodged from the ridge upon our right clattered down and roared into the lake behind us. In an instant Holmes had raced up on to the ridge, and, standing upon a lofty pinnacle, craned his neck in every direction. It was in vain that our guide assured him that a fall of stones was a common chance in the spring-time at that spot. He said nothing, but he smiled at me with the air of a man who sees the fulfillment of that which he had expected.

And yet for all his watchfulness he was never depressed. On the contrary, I can never recollect having seen him in such exuberant spirits. Again and again he recurred to the fact that if he could be assured that society was freed from Professor Moriarty he would cheerfully bring his own career to a conclusion.

'I think that I may go so far as to say, Watson, that I have not lived wholly in vain,' he remarked. 'If my record were closed to-night I could still survey it with equanimity. The air of London is the sweeter for my presence. In over a thousand cases I am not aware that I have ever used my powers upon the wrong side. Of late I have been tempted to look into the problems furnished by nature rather than those more superficial ones for which our artificial state of society is responsible. Your memoirs will draw to an end, Watson, upon the day that I crown my career by the capture or extinction of the most dangerous and capable criminal in Europe.'

I shall be brief, and yet exact, in the little which remains for me to tell. It is not a subject on which I would willingly dwell, and yet I am conscious that a duty devolves upon me to omit no detail.

It was on the 3rd of May that we reached the little village of Meiringen, where we put up at the Englischer Hof, then kept by Peter Steiler the elder. Our landlord was an intelligent man, and spoke excellent English, having served for three years as waiter at the Grosvenor Hotel in London. At his advice, on the afternoon of the 4th we set off together, with the intention of crossing the hills and spending the night at the hamlet of Rosenlaui. We had strict injunctions, however, on no account to pass the falls of Reichenbach, which are about halfway up the hill, without making a small detour to see them.

It is, indeed, a fearful place. The torrent, swollen by the melting snow, plunges into a tremendous abyss from which the spray rolls up like the smoke from a burning house. The shaft into which the river hurls itself is an immense chasm, lined by glistening coal-black rock, and narrowing into a creaming, boiling pit of incalculable depth, which brims over and shoots the stream onward over its jagged lip. The long sweep of green water roaring forever down, and the thick flickering curtain of spray hissing forever upward, turn a man giddy with their constant whirl and clamour. We stood near the edge peering down at the gleam of the breaking water far below us against the black rocks and listening to the half-human shout which came booming up with the spray out of the abyss.

The path has been cut halfway round the fall to afford a complete view, but it ends abruptly, and the traveller has to return as he came. We had turned to do so, when we saw a Swiss lad come running along it with a letter in his hand. It bore the mark of the hotel which we had just left and was addressed to me by the landlord. It appeared that within a very few minutes of our leaving, an English lady had arrived who was in the last stage of consumption. She had wintered at Davos Platz and was journeying now to join her friends at Lucerne, when a sudden hemorrhage had overtaken her. It was thought that she could hardly live a few hours, but it would be a great consolation to her to see an English doctor, and, if I would only return, etc. The good Steiler assured me in a postscript that he would himself look upon my compliance as a very great favour, since the lady absolutely refused to see a Swiss physician, and he could not but feel that he was incurring a great responsibility.

The appeal was one which could not be ignored. It was impossible to refuse the request of a fellow-countrywoman dying in a strange land. Yet I had my scruples about leaving Holmes. It was finally agreed, however, that he should retain the young Swiss messenger with him as guide and companion while I returned to Meiringen. My friend would stay some little time at the fall, he said, and would then walk slowly over the hill to Rosenlaui, where I was to rejoin him in the evening. As I turned away I saw Holmes, with his back against a rock and his arms folded, gazing down at the rush of the waters. It was the last that I was ever destined to see of him in this world.

When I was near the bottom of the descent I looked back. It was impossible, from that position, to see the fall, but I could see the curving path which winds over the shoulder of the hill and leads to it. Along this a man was, I remember, walking very rapidly.

I could see his black figure clearly outlined against the green behind him. I noted him, and the energy with which he walked but he passed from my mind again as I hurried on upon my errand.

It may have been a little over an hour before I reached Meiringen. Old Steiler was standing at the porch of his hotel.

'Well,' said I, as I came hurrying up, 'I trust that she is no worse?'

A look of surprise passed over his face, and at the first quiver of his eyebrows my heart turned to lead in my breast.

'You did not write this?' I said, pulling the letter from my pocket. 'There is no sick Englishwoman in the hotel?'

'Certainly not!' he cried. 'But it has the hotel mark upon it! Ha, it must have been written by that tall Englishman who came in after you had gone. He said—'

But I waited for none of the landlord's explanations. In a

tingle of fear I was already running down the village street, and making for the path which I had so lately descended. It had taken me an hour to come down. For all my efforts two more had passed before I found myself at the fall of Reichenbach once more. There was Holmes' Alpine-stock still leaning against the rock by which I had left him. But there was no sign of him, and it was in vain that I shouted. My only answer was my own voice reverberating in a rolling echo from the cliffs around me.

It was the sight of that Alpine-stock which turned me cold and sick. He had not gone to Rosenlaui, then. He had remained on that three-foot path, with sheer wall on one side and sheer drop on the other, until his enemy had overtaken him. The young Swiss had gone too. He had probably been in the pay of Moriarty and had left the two men together. And then what had happened? Who was to tell us what had happened then?

I stood for a minute or two to collect myself, for I was dazed with the horror of the thing. Then I began to think of Holmes' own methods and to try to practise them in reading this tragedy. It was, alas, only too easy to do. During our conversation we had not gone to the end of the path, and the Alpine-stock marked the place where we had stood. The blackish soil is kept forever soft by the incessant drift of spray, and a bird would leave its tread upon it. Two lines of footmarks were clearly marked along the farther end of the path, both leading away from me. There were none returning. A few yards from the end the soil was all ploughed up into a patch of mud, and the branches and ferns which fringed the chasm were torn and bedraggled. I lay upon my face and peered over with the spray spouting up all around me. It had darkened since I left, and now I could only see here and there the glistening of moisture upon the black walls, and far away down at the end of the shaft the gleam of the broken water. I shouted, but only the same half-human cry of the fall was borne back to my ears.

But it was destined that I should after all have a last word of greeting from my friend and comrade. I have said that his Alpine-stock had been left leaning against a rock which jutted on to the path. From the top of this bowlder the gleam of something bright caught my eye, and, raising my hand, I found that it came from the silver cigarette-case which he used to carry. As I took it up a small square of paper upon which it had lain fluttered down on to the ground. Unfolding it, I found that it consisted of three pages torn from his note-book and addressed to me. It was characteristic of the man that the direction was precise, and the writing as firm and clear, as though it had been written in his study.

My dear Watson [it said], I write these few lines through the courtesy of Mr Moriarty, who awaits my convenience for the final discussion of those questions which lie between us. He has been giving me a sketch of the methods by which he avoided the English police and kept himself informed of our movements.

They certainly confirm the very high opinion which I had formed of his abilities. I am pleased to think that I shall be able to free society from any further effects of his presence, though I fear that it is at a cost which will give pain to my friends, and especially, my dear Watson, to you. I have already explained to you, however, that my career had in any case reached its crisis, and that no possible conclusion to it could be more congenial to me than this. Indeed, if I may make a full confession to you, I was quite convinced that the letter from Meiringen was a hoax, and I allowed you to depart on that errand under the persuasion that some development of this sort would follow. Tell Inspector Patterson that the papers which he needs to convict the gang are in pigeonhole M., done up in a blue envelope and inscribed 'Moriarty.' I made every disposition of my property before leaving England, and handed it to my brother Mycroft. Pray give my greetings to Mrs Watson, and believe me to be, my dear fellow,

Very sincerely yours,
Sherlock Holmes

A few words may suffice to tell the little that remains. An examination by experts leaves little doubt that a personal contest between the two men ended, as it could hardly fail to end in such a situation, in their reeling over, locked in each other's arms. Any attempt at recovering the bodies was absolutely hopeless, and there, deep down in that dreadful cauldron of swirling water and seething foam, will lie for all time the most dangerous criminal and the foremost champion of the law of their generation. The Swiss youth was never found again, and there can be no doubt that he was one of the numerous agents whom Moriarty kept in his employ. As to the gang, it will be within the memory of the public how completely the evidence which Holmes had accumulated exposed their organization, and how heavily the hand of the dead man weighed upon them. Of their terrible chief few details came out during the proceedings, and if I have now been compelled to make a clear statement of his career it is due to those injudicious champions who have endeavoured to clear his memory by attacks upon him whom I shall ever regard as the best and the wisest man whom I have ever known.

the adventure of the empty house

It was in the spring of the year 1894 that all London was interested, and the fashionable world dismayed, by the murder of the Honourable Ronald Adair under most unusual and inexplicable circumstances. The public has already learned those particulars of the crime which came out in the police investigation; but a good deal was suppressed upon that occasion, since the case for the prosecution was so overwhelmingly strong that it was not necessary to bring forward all the facts. Only now, at the end of nearly ten years, am I allowed to supply those missing links which make up the whole of that remarkable chain. The crime was of interest in itself, but that interest was nothing to me compared to the inconceivable sequel, which afforded me the greatest shock and surprise of any event in my adventurous life. Even now, after this long interval, I find myself thrilling as I think of it, and feeling once more that sudden flood of joy, amazement, and incredulity which utterly submerged my mind. Let me say to that public which has shown some interest in those glimpses which I have occasionally given them of the thoughts and actions of a very remarkable man that they are not to blame me if I have not shared my knowledge with them, for I should have considered it my first duty to have done so had I not been barred by a positive prohibition from his own lips, which was only withdrawn upon the third of last month.

It can be imagined that my close intimacy with Sherlock Holmes had interested me deeply in crime, and that after his disappearance I never failed to read with care the various problems which came before the public, and I even attempted more than once for my own private satisfaction to employ his methods in their solution, though with indifferent success. There was none, however, which appealed to me like this tragedy of Ronald Adair. As I read the evidence at the inquest, which led up to a verdict of willful murder against some person or persons, I realized more clearly than I had ever done the loss which the community had sustained by the death of Sherlock Holmes. There were points about this strange business which would, I was sure, have specially appealed to him, and the efforts of the police would have been supplemented, or more probably anticipated, by the trained observation and the alert mind of the first criminal agent in Europe. All day as I drove upon my round I turned over the case in my mind, and found no explanation which appeared to me to be adequate. At the risk of telling a twice-told tale I will recapitulate the facts as they were known to the public at the conclusion of the inquest.

The Honourable Ronald Adair was the second son of the Earl of Maynooth, at that time Governor of one of the Australian Colonies. Adair's mother had returned from Australia to undergo the operation for cataract, and she, her son Ronald, and her daughter Hilda were living together at 427, Park Lane. The youth moved in the best society, had, so far as was known, no enemies, and no particular vices. He had been engaged to Miss Edith Woodley, of Carstairs, but the engagement had been broken off by mutual consent some months before, and there was no sign that it had left any very profound feeling behind it. For the rest the man's life moved in a narrow and conventional circle, for his habits were quiet and his nature unemotional. Yet it was upon this easy-going young aristocrat that death came in most strange and unexpected form between the hours of ten and eleven-twenty on the night of March 30, 1894.

Ronald Adair was fond of cards, playing continually, but never for such stakes as would hurt him. He was a member of the Baldwin, the Cavendish, and the Bagatelle card clubs. It was shown that after dinner on the day of his death he had played a rubber of whist at the latter club. He had also played there in the afternoon. The evidence of those who had played with him—Mr Murray, Sir John Hardy, and Colonel Moran—showed that the game was whist, and that there was a fairly equal fall of the cards. Adair might have lost five pounds, but not more. His fortune was a considerable one, and such a loss could not in any way affect him. He had played nearly every day at one club or other, but he was a cautious player, and usually rose a winner. It came out in evidence that in partnership with Colonel Moran he had actually won as much as four hundred and twenty pounds in a sitting some weeks before from Godfrey Milner and Lord Balmoral. So much for his recent history, as it came out at the inquest.

On the evening of the crime he returned from the club exactly at ten. His mother and sister were out spending the evening with a relation. The servant deposed that she heard him enter the front room on the second floor, generally used as his sitting-room. She had lit a fire there, and as it smoked she had opened the window. No sound was heard from the room until eleven-twenty, the hour of the return of Lady Maynooth and her daughter. Desiring to say good-night, she had attempted to enter her son's room. The door was locked on the inside, and no answer could be got to their cries and knocking. Help was obtained and the door forced. The unfortunate young man was found lying near the table. His head had been horribly mutilated by an expanding revolver bullet, but no weapon of any sort was to be found in the room. On the table lay two bank-notes for ten pounds each and seventeen pounds ten in silver and gold, the money arranged in little piles of varying amount. There were some figures also upon a sheet of paper with the names of some club friends opposite to them, from which it was conjectured that before his death he was endeavouring to make out his losses or winnings at cards.

A minute examination of the circumstances served only to make the case more complex. In the first place, no reason could be given why the young man should have fastened the door upon the inside. There was the possibility that the murderer had done this and had afterwards escaped by the window. The drop was at least twenty feet, however, and a bed of crocuses in full bloom lay beneath. Neither the flowers nor the earth showed any sign of having been disturbed, nor were there any marks upon the narrow strip of grass which separated the house from the road.

Apparently, therefore, it was the young man himself who had fastened the door. But how did he come by his death? No one could have climbed up to the window without leaving traces. Suppose a man had fired through the window, it would indeed be a remarkable shot who could with a revolver inflict so deadly a wound. Again, Park Lane is a frequented thoroughfare, and there is a cab-stand within a hundred yards of the house. No one had heard a shot. And yet there was the dead man, and there the revolver bullet, which had mushroomed out, as soft-nosed bullets will, and so inflicted a wound which must have caused instantaneous death. Such were the circumstances of the Park Lane Mystery, which were further complicated by entire absence of motive, since, as I have said, young Adair was not known to have any enemy, and no attempt had been made to remove the money or valuables in the room.

All day I turned these facts over in my mind, endeavouring to hit upon some theory which could reconcile them all, and to find that line of least resistance which my poor friend had declared to be the starting-point of every investigation. I confess that I made little progress. In the evening I strolled across the Park, and found myself about six o'clock at the Oxford Street end of Park Lane. A group of loafers upon the pavements, all staring up at a particular window, directed me to the house which I had come to see. A tall, thin man with coloured glasses, whom I strongly suspected of being a plain-clothes detective, was pointing out some theory of his own, while the others crowded round to listen to what he said. I got as near him as I could, but his observations seemed to me to be absurd, so I withdrew again in some disgust. As I did so I struck against an elderly deformed man, who had been behind me, and I knocked down several books which he was carrying. I remember that as I picked them up I observed the title of one of them, *The Origin of Tree Worship*, and it struck me that the fellow must be some poor bibliophile who, either as a trade or as a hobby, was a collector of obscure volumes. I endeavoured to apologize for the accident, but it was evident that these books which I had so unfortunately maltreated were very precious objects in the eyes of their owner. With a snarl of contempt he turned upon his heel, and I saw his curved back and white side-whiskers disappear among the throng.

My observations of No. 427, Park Lane did little to clear up the problem in which I was interested. The house was separated from the street by a low wall and railing, the whole not more than five feet high. It was perfectly easy, therefore, for anyone to get into the garden, but the window was entirely inaccessible, since there was no water-pipe or anything which could help the most active man to climb it. More puzzled than ever I retraced my steps to Kensington. I had not been in my study five minutes when the maid entered to say that a person desired to see me. To my astonishment it was none other than my strange old book-collector, his sharp, wizened face peering out from a frame of white hair, and his precious volumes, a dozen of them at least, wedged under his right arm.

'You're surprised to see me, sir,' said he, in a strange, croaking voice.

I acknowledged that I was.

'Well, I've a conscience, sir, and when I chanced to see you go into this house, as I came hobbling after you, I thought to myself, I'll just step in and see that kind gentleman, and tell him that if I was a bit gruff in my manner there was not any harm meant, and that I am much obliged to him for picking up my books.'

'You make too much of a trifle,' said I. 'May I ask how you knew who I was?'

'Well, sir, if it isn't too great a liberty, I am a neighbour of yours, for you'll find my little bookshop at the corner of Church Street, and very happy to see you, I am sure. Maybe you collect yourself, sir; here's *British Birds*, and *Catullus*, and *The Holy War*—a bargain every one of them. With five volumes you could just fill that gap on that second shelf. It looks untidy, does it not, sir?'

I moved my head to look at the cabinet behind me. When I turned again Sherlock Holmes was standing smiling at me across my study table. I rose to my feet, stared at him for some seconds in utter amazement, and then it appears that I must have fainted for the first and the last time in my life. Certainly a grey mist swirled before my eyes, and when it cleared I found my collar-ends undone and the tingling after-taste of brandy upon my lips. Holmes was bending over my chair, his flask in his hand.

'My dear Watson,' said the well-remembered voice, 'I owe you a thousand apologies. I had no idea that you would be so affected.'

I gripped him by the arm.

'Holmes!' I cried. 'Is it really you? Can it indeed be that you are alive? Is it possible that you succeeded in climbing out of that awful abyss?'

'Wait a moment,' said he. 'Are you sure that you are really fit to discuss things? I have given you a serious shock by my unnecessarily dramatic reappearance.'

'I am all right, but indeed, Holmes, I can hardly believe my eyes. Good heavens, to think that you—you of all men—should be standing in my study!' Again I gripped him by the sleeve and felt the thin, sinewy arm beneath it. 'Well, you're not a spirit, anyhow,' said I. 'My dear chap, I am overjoyed to see you. Sit down and tell me how you came alive out of that dreadful chasm.'

He sat opposite to me and lit a cigarette in his old nonchalant manner. He was dressed in the seedy frock-coat of the book merchant, but the rest of that individual lay in a pile of white hair and old books upon the table. Holmes looked even thinner and keener than of old, but there was a dead-white tinge in his aquiline face which told me that his life recently had not been a healthy one.

'I am glad to stretch myself, Watson,' said he. 'It is no joke when a tall man has to take a foot off his stature for several hours on end. Now, my dear fellow, in the matter of these explanations, we have, if I may ask for your co-operation, a hard and dangerous night's work in front of us. Perhaps it would be better if I gave you an account of the whole situation when that work is finished.'

'I am full of curiosity. I should much prefer to hear now.'

'You'll come with me to-night?'

'When you like and where you like.'

'This is indeed like the old days. We shall have time for a mouthful of dinner before we need go. Well, then, about that chasm. I had no serious difficulty in getting out of it, for the very simple reason that I never was in it.'

'You never were in it?'

'No, Watson, I never was in it. My note to you was absolutely genuine. I had little doubt that I had come to the end of my career when I perceived the somewhat sinister figure of the late Professor Moriarty standing upon the narrow pathway which led to safety. I read an inexorable purpose in his grey eyes. I exchanged some remarks with him, therefore, and obtained his courteous permission to write the short note which you afterwards received. I left it with my cigarette-box and my stick and I walked along the pathway, Moriarty still at my heels. When I reached the end I stood at bay. He drew no weapon, but he rushed at me and threw his long arms around me. He knew that his own game was up, and was only anxious to revenge himself upon me. We tottered together upon the brink of the fall. I have some knowledge, however, of baritsu, or the Japanese system of wrestling, which has more than once been very useful to me. I slipped through his grip, and he with a horrible scream kicked madly for a few seconds and clawed the air with both his hands. But for all his efforts he could not get his balance, and over he went. With my face over the brink I saw him fall for a long way. Then he struck a rock, bounded off, and splashed into the water.'

I listened with amazement to this explanation, which Holmes delivered between the puffs of his cigarette.

'But the tracks!' I cried. 'I saw with my own eyes that two went down the path and none returned.'

'It came about in this way. The instant that the Professor had disappeared it struck me what a really extraordinarily lucky chance Fate had placed in my way. I knew that Moriarty was not the only man who had sworn my death. There were at least three others whose desire for vengeance upon me would only be increased by the death of their leader. They were all most dangerous men. One or other would certainly get me. On the other hand, if all the world was convinced that I was dead they would take liberties, these men, they would lay themselves open, and sooner or later I could destroy them. Then it would be time for me to announce that I was still in the land of the living. So rapidly does the brain act that I believe I had thought this all out before Professor Moriarty had reached the bottom of the Reichenbach Fall.

'I stood up and examined the rocky wall behind me. In your picturesque account of the matter, which I read with great interest some months later, you assert that the wall was sheer. This was not literally true. A few small footholds presented themselves, and there was some indication of a ledge. The cliff is so high that to climb it all was an obvious impossibility, and it was equally impossible to make my way along the wet path without leaving some tracks. I might, it is true, have reversed my boots, as I have done on similar occasions, but the sight of three sets of tracks in one direction would certainly have suggested a deception. On the whole, then, it was best that I should risk the climb. It was not a pleasant business, Watson. The fall roared beneath me. I am not a fanciful person, but I give you my word that I seemed to hear Moriarty's voice screaming at me out of the abyss. A mistake would have been fatal. More than once, as tufts of grass came out in my hand or my foot slipped in the wet notches of the rock, I thought that I was gone. But I struggled upwards, and at last I reached a ledge several feet deep and covered with soft green moss, where I could lie unseen in the most perfect comfort. There I was stretched when you, my dear Watson, and all your following were investigating in the most sympathetic and inefficient manner the circumstances of my death.

'At last, when you had all formed your inevitable and totally erroneous conclusions, you departed for the hotel and I was left alone. I had imagined that I had reached the end of my adventures, but a very unexpected occurrence showed me that there were surprises still in store for me. A huge rock, falling from above, boomed past me, struck the path, and bounded over into the chasm. For an instant I thought that it was an accident; but a moment later, looking up, I saw a man's head against the darkening sky, and another stone struck the very ledge upon which I was stretched, within a foot of my head. Of course, the meaning of this was obvious. Moriarty had not been alone. A confederate—and even that one glance had told me how dangerous a man that confederate was—had kept guard while the Professor had attacked me. From a distance, unseen by me, he had been a witness of his friend's death and of my escape. He had waited, and then, making his way round to the top of the cliff, he had endeavoured to succeed where his comrade had failed.

'I did not take long to think about it, Watson. Again I saw that grim face look over the cliff, and I knew that it was the precursor of another stone. I scrambled down on to the path. I don't think I could have done it in cold blood. It was a hundred times more difficult than getting up. But I had no time to think of the danger, for another stone sang past me as I hung by my hands from the edge of the ledge. Halfway down I slipped, but by the blessing of God I landed, torn and bleeding, upon the path. I took to my heels, did ten miles over the mountains in the darkness, and a week later I found myself in Florence with the certainty that no one in the world knew what had become of me.

'I had only one confidant—my brother Mycroft. I owe you many apologies, my dear Watson, but it was all-important that it should be thought I was dead, and it is quite certain that you would not have written so convincing an account of my unhappy end had you not yourself thought that it was true. Several times during the last three years I have taken up my pen to write to you, but always I feared lest your affectionate regard for me should tempt you to some indiscretion which would betray my secret. For that reason I turned away from you this evening when you upset my books, for I was in danger at the time, and any show of surprise and emotion upon your part might have drawn attention to my identity and led to the most deplorable and irreparable results. As to Mycroft, I had to confide in him in order to obtain the money which I needed. The course of events in London did not run so well as I had hoped, for the trial of the Moriarty gang left two of its most dangerous members, my own most vindictive enemies, at liberty. I travelled for two years in Tibet, therefore, and amused myself by visiting Lhasa and spending some days with the head Llama. You may have read of the remarkable explorations of a Norwegian named Sigerson, but I am sure that it never occurred to you that you were receiving news of your friend. I then passed through Persia, looked in at Mecca, and paid a short but interesting visit to the Khalifa at Khartoum, the results of which I have communicated to the Foreign Office. Returning to France I spent some months in a research into the coal-tar derivatives, which I conducted in a laboratory at Montpelier, in the South of France. Having concluded this to my satisfaction, and learning that only one of my enemies was now left in London, I was about to return when my movements were hastened by the news of this very remarkable Park Lane Mystery, which not only appealed to me by its own merits, but which seemed to offer some most peculiar personal opportunities. I came over at once to London, called in my own person at Baker Street, threw Mrs Hudson into violent hysterics, and found that Mycroft had preserved my rooms and my papers exactly as they had always been. So it was, my dear Watson, that at two o'clock to-day I found myself in my old arm-chair in my own old room, and only wishing that I could have seen my old friend Watson in the other chair which he has so often adorned.'

Such was the remarkable narrative to which I listened on that April evening—a narrative which would have been utterly incredible to me had it not been confirmed by the actual sight of the tall, spare figure and the keen, eager face, which I had never thought to see again. In some manner he had learned of my own sad bereavement, and his sympathy was shown in his manner rather than in his words. 'Work is the best antidote to sorrow, my dear Watson,' said he, 'and I have a piece of work for us both to-night which, if we can bring it to a successful conclusion, will in itself justify a man's life on this planet.' In vain I begged him to tell me more. 'You will hear and see enough before morning,' he answered. 'We have three years of the past to discuss. Let that suffice until half-past nine, when we start upon the notable adventure of the empty house.'

It was indeed like old times when, at that hour, I found myself seated beside him in a hansom, my revolver in my pocket and the thrill of adventure in my heart. Holmes was cold and stern and silent. As the gleam of the street-lamps flashed upon his austere features I saw that his brows were drawn down in thought and his thin lips compressed. I knew not what wild beast we were about to hunt down in the dark jungle of criminal London, but I was well assured from the bearing of this master huntsman that the adventure was a most grave one, while the sardonic smile which occasionally broke through his ascetic gloom boded little good for the object of our quest.

I had imagined that we were bound for Baker Street, but Holmes stopped the cab at the corner of Cavendish Square. I observed that as he stepped out he gave a most searching glance to right and left, and at every subsequent street corner he took the utmost pains to assure that he was not followed. Our route was certainly a singular one. Holmes' knowledge of the byways of London was extraordinary, and on this occasion he passed rapidly, and with an assured step, through a network of mews and stables the very existence of which I had never known. We emerged at last into a small road, lined with old, gloomy houses, which led us into Manchester Street, and so to Blandford Street. Here he turned swiftly down a narrow passage, passed through a wooden gate into a deserted yard, and then opened with a key the back door of a house. We entered together and he closed it behind us.

The place was pitch-dark, but it was evident to me that it was an empty house. Our feet creaked and crackled over the bare planking, and my outstretched hand touched a wall from which the paper was hanging in ribbons. Holmes' cold, thin fingers closed round my wrist and led me forwards down a long hall, until I dimly saw the murky fanlight over the door. Here Holmes turned suddenly to the right, and we found ourselves in a large, square, empty room, heavily shadowed in the corners, but faintly lit in the centre from the lights of the street beyond. There was no lamp near and the window was thick with dust, so that we could only just discern each other's figures within. My companion put his hand upon my shoulder and his lips close to my ear.

'Do you know where we are?' he whispered.

'Surely that is Baker Street,' I answered, staring through the dim window.

'Exactly. We are in Camden House, which stands opposite to our own old quarters.'

'But why are we here?'

'Because it commands so excellent a view of that picturesque pile. Might I trouble you, my dear Watson, to draw a little nearer to the window, taking every precaution not to show yourself, and then to look up at our old rooms—

the starting-point of so many of our little adventures? We will see if my three years of absence have entirely taken away my power to surprise you.'

I crept forward and looked across at the familiar window. As my eyes fell upon it I gave a gasp and a cry of amazement. The blind was down and a strong light was burning in the room. The shadow of a man who was seated in a chair within was thrown in hard, black outline upon the luminous screen of the window. There was no mistaking the poise of the head, the squareness of the shoulders, the sharpness of the features. The face was turned half-round, and the effect was that of one of those black silhouettes which our grandparents loved to frame. It was a perfect reproduction of Holmes. So amazed was I that I threw out my hand to make sure that the man himself was standing beside me. He was quivering with silent laughter.

'Well?' said he.

'Good heavens!' I cried. 'It is marvellous.'

'I trust that age doth not wither nor custom stale my infinite variety,' said he, and I recognized in his voice the joy and pride which the artist takes in his own creation. 'It really is rather like me, is it not?'

'I should be prepared to swear that it was you.'

'The credit of the execution is due to Monsieur Oscar Meunier, of Grenoble, who spent some days in doing the moulding. It is a bust in wax. The rest I arranged myself during my visit to Baker Street this afternoon.'

'But why?'

'Because, my dear Watson, I had the strongest possible reason for wishing certain people to think that I was there when I was really elsewhere.'

'And you thought the rooms were watched?'

'I *knew* that they were watched.'

'By whom?'

'By my old enemies, Watson. By the charming society whose leader lies in the Reichenbach Fall. You must remember that they knew, and only they knew, that I was still alive. Sooner or later they believed that I should come back to my rooms. They watched them continuously, and this morning they saw me arrive.'

'How do you know?'

'Because I recognized their sentinel when I glanced out of my window. He is a harmless enough fellow, Parker by name, a garroter by trade, and a remarkable performer upon the Jew's harp. I cared nothing for him. But I cared a great deal for the much more formidable person who was behind him, the bosom friend of Moriarty, the man who dropped the rocks over the cliff, the most cunning and dangerous criminal in London. That is the man who is after me to-night, Watson, and that is the man who is quite unaware that we are after *him*.'

My friend's plans were gradually revealing themselves. From this convenient retreat the watchers were being watched and the trackers tracked. That angular shadow up yonder was the bait and we were the hunters. In silence we stood together in the darkness and watched the hurrying figures who passed and repassed in front of us. Holmes was silent and motionless; but I could tell that he was keenly alert, and that his eyes were fixed intently upon the stream of passers-by. It was a bleak and boisterous night, and the wind whistled shrilly down the long street. Many people were moving to and fro, most of them muffled in their coats and cravats. Once or twice it seemed to me that I had seen the same figure before, and I especially noticed two men who appeared to be sheltering themselves from the wind in the doorway of a house some distance up the street. I tried to draw my companion's attention to them, but he gave a little ejaculation of impatience and continued to stare into the street. More than once he fidgeted with his feet and tapped rapidly with his fingers upon the wall. It was evident to me that he was becoming uneasy and that his plans were not working out altogether as he had hoped. At last, as midnight approached and the street gradually cleared, he paced up and down the room in uncontrollable agitation. I was about to make some remark to him when I raised my eyes to the lighted window and again experienced almost as great a surprise as before. I clutched Holmes' arm and pointed upwards.

'The shadow has moved!' I cried.

It was, indeed, no longer the profile, but the back, which was turned towards us.

Three years had certainly not smoothed the asperities of his temper or his impatience with a less active intelligence than his own.

'Of course it has moved,' said he. 'Am I such a farcical bungler, Watson, that I should erect an obvious dummy and expect that some of the sharpest men in Europe would be deceived by it? We have been in this room two hours, and Mrs Hudson has made some change in that figure eight times, or once in every quarter of an hour. She works it from the front so that her shadow may never be seen. Ah!' He drew in his breath with a shrill, excited intake. In the dim light I saw his head thrown forward, his whole attitude rigid with attention. Outside, the street was absolutely deserted. Those two men might still be crouching in the doorway, but I could no longer see them. All was still and dark, save only that brilliant yellow screen in front of us with the black figure outlined upon its centre. Again in the utter silence I heard that thin, sibilant note which spoke of intense suppressed excitement. An instant later he pulled me back into the blackest corner of the room, and I felt his warning hand upon my lips. The fingers which clutched me were quivering. Never had I known my friend more moved, and yet the dark street still stretched lonely and motionless before us.

But suddenly I was aware of that which his keener senses had already distinguished. A low, stealthy sound came to my ears, not from the direction of Baker Street, but from the back of the very house in which we lay concealed. A door opened and shut. An instant later steps crept down the passage steps which were meant to be silent, but which reverberated harshly through the empty house. Holmes crouched back against the wall and I did the same, my hand closing upon the handle of my revolver. Peering through the gloom, I saw the vague outline of a man, a shade blacker than the blackness of the open door. He stood for an instant, and then he crept forward, crouching, menacing, into the room. He was within three yards of us, this sinister figure, and I had braced myself to meet his spring, before I realized that he had no idea of our presence. He passed close beside us, stole over to the window, and very softly and noiselessly raised it for half a foot. As he sank to the level of this opening, the light of the street, no longer dimmed by the dusty glass, fell full upon his face. The man seemed to be beside himself with excitement. His two eyes shone like stars and his features were working convulsively. He was an elderly man, with a thin, projecting nose, a high, bald forehead, and a huge grizzled moustache. An opera-hat was pushed to the back of his head, and an evening dress shirt-front gleamed out through his open overcoat. His face was gaunt and swarthy, scored with deep, savage lines. In his hand he carried what appeared to be a stick, but as he laid it down upon the floor it gave a metallic clang. Then from the pocket of his overcoat he drew a bulky object, and he busied himself in some task which ended with a loud, sharp click, as if a spring or bolt had fallen into its place. Still kneeling upon the floor he bent forward and threw all his weight and strength upon some lever, with the result that there came a long, whirling, grinding noise, ending once more in a powerful click. He straightened himself then, and I saw that what he held in his hand was a sort of gun, with a curiously misshapen butt. He opened it at the breech, put something in, and snapped the breech-block. Then, crouching down, he rested the end of the barrel upon the ledge of the open window, and I saw his long moustache droop over the stock and his eye gleam as it peered along the sights. I heard a little sigh of satisfaction as he cuddled the butt into his shoulder, and saw that amazing target, the black man on the yellow ground, standing clear at the end of his fore sight. For an instant he was rigid and motionless. Then his finger tightened on the trigger. There was a strange, loud whiz and a long, silvery tinkle of broken glass. At that instant Holmes sprang like a tiger on to the marksman's back and hurled him flat upon his face. He was up again in a moment, and with convulsive strength he seized Holmes by the throat; but I struck him on the head with the butt of my revolver and he dropped again upon the floor. I fell upon him, and as I held him my comrade blew a shrill call upon a whistle. There was the clatter of running feet upon the pavement, and two policemen in uniform, with one plain-clothes detective, rushed through the front entrance and into the room.

'That you, Lestrade?' said Holmes.

'Yes, Mr Holmes. I took the job myself. It's good to see you back in London, sir.'

'I think you want a little unofficial help. Three undetected murders in one year won't do, Lestrade. But you handled the Molesey Mystery with less than your usual—that's to say, you handled it fairly well.'

We had all risen to our feet, our prisoner breathing hard, with a stalwart constable on each side of him. Already a few loiterers had begun to collect in the street. Holmes stepped up to the window, closed it, and dropped the blinds. Lestrade had produced two candles and the policemen had uncovered their lanterns. I was able at last to have a good look at our prisoner.

It was a tremendously virile and yet sinister face which was turned towards us. With the brow of a philosopher above and the jaw of a sensualist below, the man must have started with great capacities for good or for evil. But one could not look upon his cruel blue eyes, with their drooping, cynical lids, or upon the fierce, aggressive nose and the threatening, deep-lined brow, without reading Nature's plainest danger-signals. He took no heed of any of us, but his eyes were fixed upon Holmes' face with an expression in which hatred and amazement were equally blended. 'You fiend!' he kept on muttering. 'You clever, clever fiend!'

'Ah, Colonel!' said Holmes, arranging his rumpled collar; '"journeys end in lovers' meetings," as the old play says. I don't think I have had the pleasure of seeing you since you favoured me with those attentions as I lay on the ledge above the Reichenbach Fall.'

The Colonel still stared at my friend like a man in a trance. 'You cunning, cunning fiend!' was all that he could say.

'I have not introduced you yet,' said Holmes. 'This, gentlemen, is Colonel Sebastian Moran, once of Her Majesty's Indian Army, and the best heavy game shot that our Eastern Empire has ever produced. I believe I am correct, Colonel, in saying that your bag of tigers still remains unrivalled?'

The fierce old man said nothing, but still glared at my companion; with his savage eyes and bristling moustache he was wonderfully like a tiger himself.

'I wonder that my very simple stratagem could deceive so old a shikari,' said Holmes. 'It must be very familiar to you. Have you not tethered a young kid under a tree, lain above it with your rifle, and waited for the bait to bring up your tiger? This empty house is my tree and you are my tiger. You have possibly had other guns in reserve in case there should be several tigers, or in the unlikely supposition of your own aim failing you. These,' he pointed around, 'are my other guns. The parallel is exact.'

Colonel Moran sprang forward, with a snarl of rage, but the constables dragged him back. The fury upon his face was terrible to look at.

'I confess that you had one small surprise for me,' said Holmes. 'I did not anticipate that you would yourself make use of this empty house and this convenient front window. I had imagined you as operating from the street, where my friend Lestrade and his merry men were awaiting you. With that exception all has gone as I expected.'

Colonel Moran turned to the official detective.

'You may or may not have just cause for arresting me,' said he, 'but at least there can be no reason why I should submit to the gibes of this person. If I am in the hands of the law let things be done in a legal way.'

'Well, that's reasonable enough,' said Lestrade. 'Nothing further you have to say, Mr Holmes, before we go?'

Holmes had picked up the powerful air-gun from the floor and was examining its mechanism. 'An admirable and unique weapon,' said he, 'noiseless and of tremendous power. I knew Von Herder, the blind German mechanic, who constructed it to the order of the late Professor Moriarty. For years I have been aware of its existence, though I have never before had the opportunity of handling it. I commend it very specially to your attention, Lestrade, and also the bullets which fit it.'

'You can trust us to look after that, Mr Holmes,' said Lestrade, as the whole party moved towards the door. 'Anything further to say?'

'Only to ask what charge you intend to prefer?'

'What charge, sir? Why, of course, the attempted murder of Mr Sherlock Holmes.'

'Not so, Lestrade. I do not propose to appear in the matter at all. To you, and to you only, belongs the credit of the remarkable arrest which you have effected. Yes, Lestrade, I congratulate you! With your usual happy mixture of cunning and audacity you have got him.'

'Got him! Got whom, Mr Holmes?'

'The man that the whole force has been seeking in vain Colonel Sebastian Moran, who shot the Honourable Ronald Adair with an expanding bullet from an air-gun through the open window of the second-floor front of No. 427, Park Lane, upon the 30th of last month. That's the charge, Lestrade. And now, Watson, if you can endure the draught from a broken window, I think that half an hour in my study over a cigar may afford you some profitable amusement.'

Our old chambers had been left unchanged through the supervision of Mycroft Holmes and the immediate care of Mrs Hudson. As I entered I saw, it is true, an unwonted tidiness, but the old landmarks were all in their place. There were the chemical corner and the acid-stained, deal-topped table. There upon a shelf was the row of formidable scrap-books and books of reference which many of our fellow-citizens would have been so glad to burn. The diagrams, the violin-case, and the pipe-rack—even the Persian slipper which contained the tobacco—all met my eyes as I glanced round me. There were two occupants of the room—one Mrs Hudson, who beamed upon us both as we entered; the other the strange dummy which had played so important a part in the evening's adventures. It was a wax-coloured model of my friend, so admirably done that it was a perfect facsimile. It stood on a small pedestal table with an old dressing-gown of Holmes' so draped round it that the illusion from the street was absolutely perfect.

'I hope you preserved all precautions, Mrs Hudson?' said Holmes.

'I went to it on my knees, sir, just as you told me.'

'Excellent. You carried the thing out very well. Did you observe where the bullet went?'

'Yes, sir. I'm afraid it has spoilt your beautiful bust, for it passed right through the head and flattened itself on the wall. I picked it up from the carpet. Here it is!'

Holmes held it out to me. 'A soft revolver bullet, as you perceive, Watson. There's genius in that, for who would expect to find such a thing fired from an air-gun. All right, Mrs Hudson, I am much obliged for your assistance. And now, Watson, let me see you in your old seat once more, for there are several points which I should like to discuss with you.'

He had thrown off the seedy frock-coat, and now he was the Holmes of old in the mouse-coloured dressing-gown which he took from his effigy.

'The old shikari's nerves have not lost their steadiness nor his eyes their keenness,' said he, with a laugh, as he inspected the shattered forehead of his bust.

'Plumb in the middle of the back of the head and smack through the brain. He was the best shot in India, and I expect that there are few better in London. Have you heard the name?'

'No, I have not.'

'Well, well, such is fame! But, then, if I remember aright, you had not heard the name of Professor James Moriarty, who had one of the great brains of the century. Just give me down my index of biographies from the shelf.'

He turned over the pages lazily, leaning back in his chair and blowing great clouds from his cigar.

'My collection of M's is a fine one,' said he. 'Moriarty himself is enough to make any letter illustrious, and here is Morgan the poisoner, and Merridew of abominable memory, and Mathews, who knocked out my left canine in the waiting-room at Charing Cross, and, finally, here is our friend of to-night.'

He handed over the book, and I read: '*Moran, Sebastian, Colonel.* Unemployed. Formerly 1st Bengalore Pioneers. Born London, 1840. Son of Sir Augustus Moran, C.B., once British Minister to Persia. Educated Eton and Oxford. Served in Jowaki Campaign, Afghan Campaign, Charasiab (despatches), Sherpur, and Cabul. Author of *Heavy Game of the Western Himalayas*, 1881; *Three Months in the Jungle*, 1884. Address: Conduit Street. Clubs: The Anglo-Indian, the Tankerville, the Bagatelle Card Club.'

On the margin was written, in Holmes' precise hand: 'The second most dangerous man in London.'

'This is astonishing,' said I, as I handed back the volume. 'The man's career is that of an honourable soldier.'

'It is true,' Holmes answered. 'Up to a certain point he did well. He was always a man of iron nerve, and the story is still told in India how he crawled down a drain after a wounded man-eating tiger. There are some trees, Watson, which grow to a certain height and then suddenly develop some unsightly eccentricity. You will see it often in humans. I have a theory that the individual represents in his development the whole procession of his ancestors, and that such a sudden turn to good or evil stands for some strong influence which came into the line of his pedigree. The person becomes, as it were, the epitome of the history of his own family.'

'It is surely rather fanciful.'

'Well, I don't insist upon it. Whatever the cause, Colonel Moran began to go wrong. Without any open scandal he still made India too hot to hold him. He retired, came to London, and again acquired an evil name. It was at this time that he was sought out by Professor Moriarty, to whom for a time he was chief of the staff. Moriarty supplied him liberally with money and used him only in one or two very high-class jobs which no ordinary criminal could have undertaken. You may have some recollection of the death of Mrs Stewart, of Lauder, in 1887. Not? Well, I am sure Moran was at the bottom of it, but nothing could be proved. So cleverly was the Colonel concealed that even when the Moriarty gang was broken up we could not incriminate him. You remember at that date, when I called upon you in your rooms, how I put up the shutters for fear of air-guns? No doubt you thought me fanciful. I knew exactly what I was doing, for I knew of the existence of this remarkable gun, and I knew also that one of the best shots in the world would be behind it. When we were in Switzerland he followed us with Moriarty, and it was undoubtedly he who gave me that evil five minutes on the Reichenbach ledge.

'You may think that I read the papers with some attention during my sojourn in France, on the look-out for any chance of laying him by the heels. So long as he was free in London my life would really not have been worth living. Night and day the shadow would have been over me, and sooner or later his chance must have come. What could I do? I could not shoot him at sight, or I should myself be in the dock. There was no use appealing to a magistrate. They cannot interfere on the strength of what would appear to them to be a wild suspicion. So I could do nothing. But I watched the criminal news, knowing that sooner or later I should get him. Then came the death of this Ronald Adair. My chance had come at last! Knowing what I did, was it not certain that Colonel Moran had done it? He had played cards with the lad; he had followed him home from the club; he had shot him through the open window. There was not a doubt of it. The bullets alone are enough to put his head in a noose. I came over at once. I was seen by the sentinel, who would, I knew, direct the Colonel's attention to my presence. He could not fail to connect my sudden return with his crime and to be terribly alarmed. I was sure that he would make an attempt to get me out of the way *at once*, and would bring round his murderous weapon for that purpose. I left him an excellent mark in the window, and, having warned the police that they might be needed— by the way, Watson, you spotted their presence in that doorway with unerring accuracy—I took up what seemed to me to be a judicious post for observation, never dreaming that he would choose the same spot for his attack. Now, my dear Watson, does anything remain for me to explain?'

'Yes,' said I. 'You have not made it clear what was Colonel Moran's motive in murdering the Honourable Ronald Adair.'

'Ah! my dear Watson, there we come into those realms of conjecture where the most logical mind may be at fault. Each may form his own hypothesis upon the present evidence, and yours is as likely to be correct as mine.'

'You have formed one, then?'

'I think that it is not difficult to explain the facts. It came out in evidence that Colonel Moran and young Adair had between them won a considerable amount of money. Now, Moran undoubtedly played foul of that I have long been aware. I believe that on the day of the murder Adair had discovered that Moran was cheating. Very likely he had spoken to him privately and had threatened to expose him unless he voluntarily resigned his membership of the club and promised not to play cards again. It is unlikely that a youngster like Adair would at once make a hideous scandal by exposing a well-known man so much older than himself. Probably he acted as I suggest. The exclusion from his clubs would mean ruin to Moran, who lived by his ill-gotten card gains. He therefore murdered Adair, who at the time was endeavouring to work out how much money he should himself return, since he could not profit by his partner's foul play. He locked the door lest the ladies should surprise him and insist upon knowing what he was doing with these names and coins. Will it pass?'

'I have no doubt that you have hit upon the truth.'

'It will be verified or disproved at the trial. Meanwhile, come what may, Colonel Moran will trouble us no more, the famous air-gun of Von Herder will embellish the Scotland Yard Museum, and once again Mr Sherlock Holmes is free to devote his life to examining those interesting little problems which the complex life of London so plentifully presents.'

the five orange pips

When I glance over my notes and records of the Sherlock Holmes cases between the years '82 and '90, I am faced by so many which present strange and interesting features that it is no easy matter to know which to choose and which to leave. Some, however, have already gained publicity through the papers, and others have not offered a field for those peculiar qualities which my friend possessed in so high a degree, and which it is the object of these papers to illustrate. Some, too, have baffled his analytical skill, and would be, as narratives, beginnings without an ending, while others have been but partially cleared up, and have their explanations founded rather upon conjecture and surmise than on that absolute logical proof which was so dear to him. There is, however, one of these last which was so remarkable in its details and so startling in its results that I am tempted to give some account of it in spite of the fact that there are points in connection with it which never have been, and probably never will be, entirely cleared up.

The year '87 furnished us with a long series of cases of greater or less interest, of which I retain the records. Among my headings under this one twelve months I find an account of the adventure of the Paradol Chamber, of the Amateur Mendicant Society, who held a luxurious club in the lower vault of a furniture warehouse, of the facts connected with the loss of the British barque *Sophy Anderson*, of the singular adventures of the Grice Patersons in the island of Uffa, and finally of the Camberwell poisoning case. In the latter, as may be remembered, Sherlock Holmes was able, by winding up the dead man's watch, to prove that it had been wound up two hours before, and that therefore the deceased had gone to bed within that time, a deduction which was of the greatest importance in clearing up the case. All these I may sketch out at some future date, but none of them present such singular features as the strange train of circumstances which I have now taken up my pen to describe.

It was in the latter days of September, and the equinoctial gales had set in with exceptional violence. All day the wind had screamed and the rain had beaten against the windows, so that even here in the heart of great, hand-made London we were forced to raise our minds for the instant from the routine of life and to recognize the presence of those great elemental forces which shriek at mankind through the bars of his civilization, like untamed beasts in a cage. As evening drew in, the storm grew higher and louder, and the wind cried and sobbed like a child in the chimney. Sherlock Holmes sat moodily at one side of the fireplace cross-indexing his records of crime, while I at the other was deep in one of Clark Russell's fine sea-stories until the howl of the gale from without seemed to blend with the text, and the splash of the rain to lengthen out into the long swash of the sea waves. My wife was on a visit to her mother's, and for a few days I was a dweller once more in my old quarters at Baker Street.

'Why,' said I, glancing up at my companion, 'that was surely the bell. Who could come to-night? Some friend of yours, perhaps?'

'Except yourself I have none,' he answered. 'I do not encourage visitors.'

'A client, then?'

'If so, it is a serious case. Nothing less would bring a man out on such a day and at such an hour. But I take it that it is more likely to be some crony of the landlady's.'

Sherlock Holmes was wrong in his conjecture, however, for there came a step in the passage and a tapping at the door. He stretched out his long arm to turn the lamp away from himself and towards the vacant chair upon which a newcomer must sit.

'Come in!' said he.

The man who entered was young, some two-and-twenty at the outside, well-groomed and trimly clad, with something of refinement and delicacy in his bearing. The streaming umbrella which he held in his hand, and his long shining waterproof told of the fierce weather through which he had come. He looked about him anxiously in the glare of the lamp, and I could see that his face was pale and his eyes heavy, like those of a man who is weighed down with some great anxiety.

'I owe you an apology,' he said, raising his golden pince-nez to his eyes. 'I trust that I am not intruding. I fear that I have brought some traces of the storm and rain into your snug chamber.'

'Give me your coat and umbrella,' said Holmes. 'They may rest here on the hook and will be dry presently. You have come up from the south-west, I see.'

'Yes, from Horsham.'

'That clay and chalk mixture which I see upon your toe caps is quite distinctive.'

'I have come for advice.'

'That is easily got.'

'And help.'

'That is not always so easy.'

'I have heard of you, Mr Holmes. I heard from Major Prendergast how you saved him in the Tankerville Club scandal.'

'Ah, of course. He was wrongfully accused of cheating at cards.'

'He said that you could solve anything.'

'He said too much.'

'That you are never beaten.'

'I have been beaten four times—three times by men, and once by a woman.'

'But what is that compared with the number of your successes?'

'It is true that I have been generally successful.'

'Then you may be so with me.'

'I beg that you will draw your chair up to the fire and favour me with some details as to your case.'

'It is no ordinary one.'

'None of those which come to me are. I am the last court of appeal.'

'And yet I question, sir, whether, in all your experience, you have ever listened to a more mysterious and inexplicable chain of events than those which have happened in my own family.'

'You fill me with interest,' said Holmes. 'Pray give us the essential facts from the commencement, and I can afterwards question you as to those details which seem to me to be most important.'

The young man pulled his chair up and pushed his wet feet out towards the blaze.

'My name,' said he, 'is John Openshaw, but my own affairs have, as far as I can understand, little to do with this awful business. It is a hereditary matter; so in order to give you an idea of the facts, I must go back to the commencement of the affair.

'You must know that my grandfather had two sons—my uncle Elias and my father Joseph. My father had a small factory at Coventry, which he enlarged at the time of the invention of bicycling. He was a patentee of the Openshaw unbreakable tire, and his business met with such success that he was able to sell it and to retire upon a handsome competence.

'My uncle Elias emigrated to America when he was a young man and became a planter in Florida, where he was reported to have done very well. At the time of the war he fought in Jackson's army, and afterwards under Hood, where he rose to be a colonel. When Lee laid down his arms my uncle returned to his plantation, where he remained for three or four years. About 1869 or 1870 he came back to Europe and took a small estate in Sussex, near Horsham. He had made a very considerable fortune in the States, and his reason for leaving them was his aversion to the negroes, and his dislike of the Republican policy in extending the franchise to them. He was a singular man, fierce and quick-tempered, very foul-mouthed when he was angry, and of a most retiring disposition. During all the years that he lived at Horsham, I doubt if ever he set foot in the town. He had a garden and two or three fields round his house, and there he would take his exercise, though very often for weeks on end he would never leave his room. He drank a great deal of brandy and smoked very heavily, but he would see no society and did not want any friends, not even his own brother.

'He didn't mind me; in fact, he took a fancy to me, for at the time when he saw me first I was a youngster of twelve or so. This would be in the year 1878, after he had been eight or nine years in England. He begged my father to let me live with him and he was very kind to me in his way. When he was sober he used to be fond of playing backgammon and draughts with me, and he would make me his representative both with the servants and with the tradespeople, so that by the time that I was sixteen I was quite master of the house. I kept all the keys and could go where I liked and do what I liked, so long as I did not disturb him in his privacy. There was one singular exception, however, for he had a single room, a lumber-room up among the attics, which was invariably locked, and which he would never permit either me or anyone else to enter. With a boy's curiosity I have peeped through the keyhole, but I was never able to see more than such a collection of old trunks and bundles as would be expected in such a room.

'One day—it was in March, 1883—a letter with a foreign stamp lay upon the table in front of the colonel's plate. It was not a common thing for him to receive letters, for his bills were all paid in ready money, and he had no friends of any sort. 'From India!' said he as he took it up, 'Pondicherry postmark! What can this be?' Opening it hurriedly, out there jumped five little dried orange pips, which pattered down upon his plate. I began to laugh at this, but the laugh was struck from my lips at the sight of his face. His lip had fallen, his eyes were protruding, his skin the colour of putty, and he glared at the envelope which he still held in his trembling hand, 'K. K. K.!' he shrieked, and then, 'My God, my God, my sins have overtaken me!'

'"What is it, uncle?" I cried.

'"Death," said he, and rising from the table he retired to his room, leaving me palpitating with horror. I took up the envelope and saw scrawled in red ink upon the inner flap, just above the gum, the letter K three times repeated. There was nothing else save the five dried pips. What could be the reason of his overpowering terror? I left the breakfast-table, and as I ascended the stair I met him coming down with an old rusty key, which must have belonged to the attic, in one hand, and a small brass box, like a cashbox, in the other.

'"They may do what they like, but I'll checkmate them still," said he with an oath. "Tell Mary that I shall want a fire in my room to-day, and send down to Fordham, the Horsham lawyer."

'I did as he ordered, and when the lawyer arrived I was asked to step up to the room. The fire was burning brightly, and in the grate there was a mass of black, fluffy ashes, as of burned paper, while the brass box stood open and empty beside it. As I glanced at the box I noticed, with a start, that upon the lid was printed the treble K which I had read in the morning upon the envelope.

'"I wish you, John," said my uncle, "to witness my will. I leave my estate, with all its advantages and all its disadvantages, to my brother, your father, whence it will, no doubt, descend to you. If you can enjoy it in peace, well and good! If you find you cannot, take my advice, my boy, and leave it to your deadliest enemy. I am sorry to give you such a two-edged thing, but I can't say what turn things are going to take. Kindly sign the paper where Mr Fordham shows you."

'I signed the paper as directed, and the lawyer took it away with him. The singular incident made, as you may think, the deepest impression upon me, and I pondered over it and turned it every way in my mind without being able to make anything of it. Yet I could not shake off the vague feeling of dread which it left behind, though the sensation grew less keen as the weeks passed and nothing happened to disturb the usual routine of our lives. I could see a change in my uncle, however. He drank more than ever, and he was less inclined for any sort of society. Most of his time he would spend in his room, with the door locked upon the inside, but sometimes he would emerge in a sort of drunken frenzy and would burst out of the house and tear about the garden with a revolver in his hand, screaming out that he was afraid of no man, and that he was not to be cooped up, like a sheep in a pen, by man or devil. When these hot fits were over, however, he would rush tumultuously in at the door and lock and bar it behind him, like a man who can brazen it out no longer against the terror which lies at the roots of his soul. At such times I have seen his face, even on a cold day, glisten with moisture, as though it were new raised from a basin.

'Well, to come to an end of the matter, Mr Holmes, and not to abuse your patience, there came a night when he made one of those drunken sallies from which he never came back. We found him, when we went to search for him, face downward in a little green-scummed pool, which lay at the foot of the garden. There was no sign of any violence, and the water was but two feet deep, so that the jury, having regard to his known eccentricity, brought in a verdict of "suicide". But I, who knew how he winced from the very thought of death, had much ado to persuade myself that he had gone out of his way to meet it. The matter passed, however, and my father entered into possession of the estate, and of some £14,000, which lay to his credit at the bank.'

'One moment,' Holmes interposed, 'your statement is, I foresee, one of the most remarkable to which I have ever listened. Let me have the date of the reception by your uncle of the letter, and the date of his supposed suicide.'

'The letter arrived on March 10, 1883. His death was seven weeks later, upon the night of May 2nd.'

'Thank you. Pray proceed.'

'When my father took over the Horsham property, he, at my request, made a careful examination of the attic, which had been always locked up. We found the brass box there, although its contents had been destroyed. On the inside of the cover was a paper label, with the initials of K. K. K. repeated upon it, and "Letters, memoranda, receipts, and a register" written beneath. These, we presume, indicated the nature of the papers which had been destroyed by Colonel Openshaw. For the rest, there was nothing of much importance in the attic save a great many scattered papers and note-books bearing upon my uncle's life in America. Some of them were of the war time and showed that he had done his duty well and had borne the repute of a brave soldier. Others were of a date during the reconstruction of the Southern states and were mostly concerned with politics, for he had evidently taken a strong part in opposing the carpet-bag politicians who had been sent down from the North.

'Well, it was the beginning of '84 when my father came

to live at Horsham, and all went as well as possible with us until the January of '85. On the fourth day after the new year I heard my father give a sharp cry of surprise as we sat together at the breakfast-table. There he was, sitting with a newly opened envelope in one hand and five dried orange pips in the outstretched palm of the other one. He had always laughed at what he called my cock-and-bull story about the colonel, but he looked very scared and puzzled now that the same thing had come upon himself.

'"Why, what on earth does this mean, John?" he stammered.

'My heart had turned to lead. "It is K. K. K.," said I.

'He looked inside the envelope. "So it is," he cried. "Here are the very letters. But what is this written above them?"

'"Put the papers on the sundial," I read, peeping over his shoulder.

'"What papers? What sundial?" he asked.

'"The sundial in the garden. There is no other," said I, "but the papers must be those that are destroyed."

'"Pooh!" said he, gripping hard at his courage. "We are in a civilized land here, and we can't have tomfoolery of this kind. Where does the thing come from?"

'"From Dundee," I answered, glancing at the postmark.

'"Some preposterous practical joke," said he. "What have I to do with sundials and papers? I shall take no notice of such nonsense."

'"I should certainly speak to the police," I said.

'"And be laughed at for my pains. Nothing of the sort."

'"Then let me do so?"

"'No, I forbid you. I won't have a fuss made about such nonsense."

'It was in vain to argue with him, for he was a very obstinate man. I went about, however, with a heart which was full of forebodings.

'On the third day after the coming of the letter my father went from home to visit an old friend of his, Major Freebody, who is in command of one of the forts upon Portsdown Hill. I was glad that he should go, for it seemed to me that he was farther from danger when he was away from home. In that, however, I was in error. Upon the second day of his absence I received a telegram from the major, imploring me to come at once. My father had fallen over one of the deep chalk-pits which abound in the neighbourhood, and was lying senseless, with a shattered skull. I hurried to him, but he passed away without having ever recovered his consciousness. He had, as it appears, been returning from Fareham in the twilight, and as the country was unknown to him, and the chalk-pit unfenced, the jury had no hesitation in bringing in a verdict of "death from accidental causes." Carefully as I examined every fact connected with his death, I was unable to find anything which could suggest the idea of murder. There were no signs of violence, no footmarks, no robbery, no record of strangers having been seen upon the roads. And yet I need not tell you that my mind was far from at ease, and that I was well-nigh certain that some foul plot had been woven round him.

'In this sinister way I came into my inheritance. You will ask me why I did not dispose of it? I answer, because I was well convinced that our troubles were in some way dependent upon an incident in my uncle's life, and that the danger would be as pressing in one house as in another.

'It was in January, '85, that my poor father met his end, and two years and eight months have elapsed since then. During that time I have lived happily at Horsham, and I had begun to hope that this curse had passed away from the family, and that it had ended with the last generation. I had begun to take comfort too soon, however; yesterday morning the blow fell in the very shape in which it had come upon my father.'

The young man took from his waistcoat a crumpled envelope, and turning to the table he shook out upon it five little dried orange pips.

'This is the envelope,' he continued. 'The postmark is London eastern division. Within are the very words which were upon my father's last message: "K. K. K." and then "Put the papers on the sundial."'

'What have you done?' asked Holmes.

'Nothing.'

'Nothing?'

'To tell the truth'—he sank his face into his thin, white hands—'I have felt helpless. I have felt like one of those poor rabbits when the snake is writhing towards it. I seem to be in the grasp of some resistless, inexorable evil, which no foresight and no precautions can guard against.'

'Tut! tut!' cried Sherlock Holmes. 'You must act, man, or you are lost. Nothing but energy can save you. This is no time for despair.'

'I have seen the police.'

'Ah!'

'But they listened to my story with a smile. I am convinced that the inspector has formed the opinion that the letters are all practical jokes, and that the deaths of my relations were really accidents, as the jury stated, and were not to be connected with the warnings.'

Holmes shook his clenched hands in the air. 'Incredible imbecility!' he cried.

'They have, however, allowed me a policeman, who may remain in the house with me.'

'Has he come with you to-night?'

'No. His orders were to stay in the house.'

Again Holmes raved in the air.

'Why did you come to me,' he cried, 'and, above all, why did you not come at once?'

'I did not know. It was only to-day that I spoke to Major Prendergast about my troubles and was advised by him to come to you.'

'It is really two days since you had the letter. We should have acted before this. You have no further evidence, I suppose, than that which you have placed before us—no suggestive detail which might help us?'

'There is one thing,' said John Openshaw. He rummaged in his coat pocket, and, drawing out a piece of discoloured, blue-tinted paper, he laid it out upon the table. 'I have some remembrance,' said he, 'that on the day when my uncle burned the papers I observed that the small, unburned margins which lay amid the ashes were of this particular colour. I found this single sheet upon the floor of his room, and I am inclined to think that it may be one of the papers which has, perhaps, fluttered out from among the others, and in that way has escaped destruction. Beyond the mention of pips, I do not see that it helps us much. I think myself that it is a page from some private diary. The writing is undoubtedly my uncle's.'

Holmes moved the lamp, and we both bent over the sheet of paper, which showed by its ragged edge that it had indeed been torn from a book. It was headed, 'March, 1869,' and beneath were the following enigmatical notices:

4th. Hudson came. Same old platform.

7th. Set the pips on McCauley, Paramore, and John Swain, of St Augustine.

9th. McCauley cleared.

10th. John Swain cleared.

12th. Visited Paramore. All well.

'Thank you!' said Holmes, folding up the paper and returning it to our visitor. 'And now you must on no account lose another instant. We cannot spare time even to discuss what you have told me. You must get home instantly and act.'

'What shall I do?'

'There is but one thing to do. It must be done at once.

You must put this piece of paper which you have shown us into the brass box which you have described. You must also put in a note to say that all the other papers were burned by your uncle, and that this is the only one which remains. You must assert that in such words as will carry conviction with them. Having done this, you must at once put the box out upon the sundial, as directed. Do you understand?'

'Entirely.'

'Do not think of revenge, or anything of the sort, at present. I think that we may gain that by means of the law, but we have our web to weave, while theirs is already woven. The first consideration is to remove the pressing danger which threatens you. The second is to clear up the mystery and to punish the guilty parties.'

'I thank you,' said the young man, rising and pulling on his overcoat. 'You have given me fresh life and hope. I shall certainly do as you advise.'

'Do not lose an instant. And, above all, take care of yourself in the meanwhile, for I do not think that there can be a doubt that you are threatened by a very real and imminent danger. How do you go back?'

'By train from Waterloo.'

'It is not yet nine. The streets will be crowded, so I trust that you may be in safety. And yet you cannot guard yourself too closely.'

'I am armed.'

'That is well. To-morrow I shall set to work upon your case.'

'I shall see you at Horsham, then?'

'No, your secret lies in London. It is there that I shall seek it.'

'Then I shall call upon you in a day, or in two days, with news as to the box and the papers. I shall take your advice in every particular.' He shook hands with us and took his leave. Outside the wind still screamed and the rain splashed and pattered against the windows. This strange, wild story seemed to have come to us from amid the mad elements blown in upon us like a sheet of sea-weed in a gale and now to have been reabsorbed by them once more.

Sherlock Holmes sat for some time in silence, with his head sunk forward and his eyes bent upon the red glow of the fire. Then he lit his pipe, and leaning back in his chair he watched the blue smoke-rings as they chased each other up to the ceiling.

'I think, Watson,' he remarked at last, 'that of all our cases we have had none more fantastic than this.'

'Save, perhaps, the Sign of Four.'

'Well, yes. Save, perhaps, that. And yet this John Openshaw seems to me to be walking amid even greater perils than did the Sholtos.'

'But have you,' I asked, 'formed any definite conception as to what these perils are?'

'There can be no question as to their nature,' he answered.

'Then what are they? Who is this K. K. K., and why does he pursue this unhappy family?'

Sherlock Holmes closed his eyes and placed his elbows

upon the arms of his chair, with his finger-tips together. 'The ideal reasoner,' he remarked, 'would, when he had once been shown a single fact in all its bearings, deduce from it not only all the chain of events which led up to it but also all the results which would follow from it. As Cuvier could correctly describe a whole animal by the contemplation of a single bone, so the observer who has thoroughly understood one link in a series of incidents should be able to accurately state all the other ones, both before and after. We have not yet grasped the results which the reason alone can attain to. Problems may be solved in the study which have baffled all those who have sought a solution by the aid of their senses. To carry the art, however, to its highest pitch, it is necessary that the reasoner should be able to utilize all the facts which have come to his knowledge; and this in itself implies, as you will readily see, a possession of all knowledge, which, even in these days of free education and encyclopaedias, is a somewhat rare accomplishment. It is not so impossible, however, that a man should possess all knowledge which is likely to be useful to him in his work, and this I have endeavoured in my case to do. If I remember rightly, you on one occasion, in the early days of our friendship, defined my limits in a very precise fashion.'

'Yes,' I answered, laughing. 'It was a singular document. Philosophy, astronomy, and politics were marked at zero, I remember. Botany variable, geology profound as regards the mud-stains from any region within fifty miles of town, chemistry eccentric, anatomy unsystematic, sensational literature and crime records unique, violin-player, boxer, swordsman, lawyer, and self-poisoner by cocaine and tobacco. Those, I think, were the main points of my analysis.'

Holmes grinned at the last item. 'Well,' he said, 'I say now, as I said then, that a man should keep his little brain-attic stocked with all the furniture that he is likely to use, and the rest he can put away in the lumber-room of his library, where he can get it if he wants it. Now, for such a case as the one which has been submitted to us to-night, we need certainly to muster all our resources. Kindly hand me down the letter K of the *American Encyclopaedia* which stands upon the shelf beside you. Thank you. Now let us consider the situation and see what may be deduced from it. In the first place, we may start with a strong presumption that Colonel Openshaw had some very strong reason for leaving America. Men at his time of life do not change all their habits and exchange willingly the charming climate of Florida for the lonely life of an English provincial town. His extreme love of solitude in England suggests the idea that he was in fear of someone or something, so we may assume as a working hypothesis that it was fear of someone or something which drove him from America. As to what it was he feared, we can only deduce that by considering the formidable letters which were received by himself and his successors. Did you remark the postmarks of those letters?'

'The first was from Pondicherry, the second from Dundee, and the third from London.'

'From East London. What do you deduce from that?'

'They are all seaports. That the writer was on board of a ship.'

'Excellent. We have already a clue. There can be no doubt that the probability—the strong probability—is that the writer was on board of a ship. And now let us consider another point. In the case of Pondicherry, seven weeks elapsed between the threat and its fulfilment, in Dundee it was only some three or four days. Does that suggest anything?'

'A greater distance to travel.'

'But the letter had also a greater distance to come.'

'Then I do not see the point.'

'There is at least a presumption that the vessel in which the man or men are is a sailing-ship. It looks as if they always send their singular warning or token before them when starting upon their mission. You see how quickly the deed followed the sign when it came from Dundee. If they had come from Pondicherry in a steamer they would have arrived almost as soon as their letter. But, as a matter of fact, seven weeks elapsed. I think that those seven weeks represented the difference between the mail-boat which brought the letter and the sailing vessel which brought the writer.'

'It is possible.'

'More than that. It is probable. And now you see the deadly urgency of this new case, and why I urged young Openshaw to caution. The blow has always fallen at the end of the time which it would take the senders to travel the distance. But this one comes from London, and therefore we cannot count upon delay.'

'Good God!' I cried. 'What can it mean, this relentless persecution?'

'The papers which Openshaw carried are obviously of vital importance to the person or persons in the sailing-ship. I think that it is quite clear that there must be more than one of them. A single man could not have carried out two deaths in such a way as to deceive a coroner's jury. There must have been several in it, and they must have been men of resource and determination. Their papers they mean to have, be the holder of them who it may. In this way you see K. K. K. ceases to be the initials of an individual and becomes the badge of a society.'

'But of what society?'

'Have you never,' said Sherlock Holmes, bending forward and sinking his voice, 'have you never heard of the Ku Klux Klan?'

'I never have.'

Holmes turned over the leaves of the book upon his knee. 'Here it is,' said he presently:

'"Ku Klux Klan. A name derived from the fanciful resemblance to the sound produced by cocking a rifle. This terrible secret society was formed by some ex-Confederate soldiers in the Southern states after the Civil War, and it rapidly formed local branches in different parts of the country, notably in Tennessee, Louisiana, the Carolinas, Georgia, and Florida. Its power was used for political purposes, principally for the terrorizing of the negro voters and the murdering and driving from the country of those who were opposed to its views. Its outrages were usually preceded by a warning sent to the marked man in some fantastic but generally recognized shape a sprig of oak-leaves in some parts, melon seeds or orange pips in others. On receiving this the victim might either openly abjure his former ways, or might fly from the country. If he braved the matter out, death would unfailingly come upon him, and usually in some strange and unforeseen manner. So perfect was the organization of the society, and so systematic its methods, that there is hardly a case upon record where any man succeeded in braving it with impunity, or in which any of its outrages were traced home to the perpetrators. For some years the organization flourished in spite of the efforts of the United States government and of the better classes of the community in the South. Eventually, in the year 1869, the movement rather suddenly collapsed, although there have been sporadic outbreaks of the same sort since that date."

'You will observe,' said Holmes, laying down the volume, 'that the sudden breaking up of the society was coincident with the disappearance of Openshaw from America with their papers. It may well have been cause and effect. It is no wonder that he and his family have some of the more implacable spirits upon their track. You can understand that this register and diary may implicate some of the first men in the South, and that there may be many who will not sleep easy at night until it is recovered.'

'Then the page we have seen.'

'Is such as we might expect. It ran, if I remember right,

"sent the pips to A, B, and C" that is, sent the society's warning to them. Then there are successive entries that A and B cleared, or left the country, and finally that C was visited, with, I fear, a sinister result for C. Well, I think, Doctor, that we may let some light into this dark place, and I believe that the only chance young Openshaw has in the meantime is to do what I have told him. There is nothing more to be said or to be done to-night, so hand me over my violin and let us try to forget for half an hour the miserable weather and the still more miserable ways of our fellow men.'

It had cleared in the morning, and the sun was shining with a subdued brightness through the dim veil which hangs over the great city. Sherlock Holmes was already at breakfast when I came down.

'You will excuse me for not waiting for you,' said he, 'I have, I foresee, a very busy day before me in looking into this case of young Openshaw's.'

'What steps will you take?' I asked.

'It will very much depend upon the results of my first inquiries. I may have to go down to Horsham, after all.'

'You will not go there first?'

'No, I shall commence with the City. Just ring the bell and the maid will bring up your coffee.'

As I waited, I lifted the unopened newspaper from the table and glanced my eye over it. It rested upon a heading which sent a chill to my heart.

'Holmes,' I cried, 'you are too late.'

'Ah!' said he, laying down his cup, 'I feared as much.

How was it done?' He spoke calmly, but I could see that he was deeply moved.

'My eye caught the name of Openshaw, and the heading "Tragedy Near Waterloo Bridge." Here is the account:

'"Between nine and ten last night Police-Constable Cook, of the H Division, on duty near Waterloo Bridge, heard a cry for help and a splash in the water. The night, however, was extremely dark and stormy, so that, in spite of the help of several passers-by, it was quite impossible to effect a rescue. The alarm, however, was given, and, by the aid of the water-police, the body was eventually recovered. It proved to be that of a young gentleman whose name, as it appears from an envelope which was found in his pocket, was John Openshaw, and whose residence is near Horsham. It is conjectured that he may have been hurrying down to catch the last train from Waterloo Station, and that in his haste and the extreme darkness he missed his path and walked over the edge of one of the small landing-places for river steamboats. The body exhibited no traces of violence, and there can be no doubt that the deceased had been the victim of an unfortunate accident, which should have the effect of calling the attention of the authorities to the condition of the riverside landing-stages."'

We sat in silence for some minutes, Holmes more depressed and shaken than I had ever seen him.

'That hurts my pride, Watson,' he said at last. 'It is a petty feeling, no doubt, but it hurts my pride. It becomes a personal matter with me now, and, if God sends me health, I shall set my hand upon this gang. That he should come to me for help, and that I should send him away to his death—!' He sprang from his chair and paced about the room in uncontrollable agitation, with a flush upon his sallow cheeks and a nervous clasping and unclasping of his long thin hands.

'They must be cunning devils,' he exclaimed at last. 'How could they have decoyed him down there? The Embankment is not on the direct line to the station. The bridge, no doubt, was too crowded, even on such a night, for their purpose. Well, Watson, we shall see who will win in the long run. I am going out now!'

'To the police?'

'No, I shall be my own police. When I have spun the web they may take the flies, but not before.'

All day I was engaged in my professional work, and it was late in the evening before I returned to Baker Street. Sherlock Holmes had not come back yet. It was nearly ten o'clock before he entered, looking pale and worn. He walked up to the sideboard, and tearing a piece from the loaf he devoured it voraciously, washing it down with a long draught of water.

'You are hungry,' I remarked.

'Starving. It had escaped my memory. I have had nothing since breakfast.'

'Nothing?'

'Not a bite. I had no time to think of it.'

'And how have you succeeded?'

'Well.'

'You have a clue?'

'I have them in the hollow of my hand. Young Openshaw shall not long remain unavenged. Why, Watson, let us put their own devilish trade-mark upon them. It is well thought of!'

'What do you mean?'

He took an orange from the cupboard, and tearing it to pieces he squeezed out the pips upon the table. Of these he took five and thrust them into an envelope. On the inside of the flap he wrote 'S. H. for J. O.' Then he sealed it and addressed it to 'Captain James Calhoun, Barque *Lone Star*, Savannah, Georgia.'

'That will await him when he enters port,' said he, chuckling. 'It may give him a sleepless night. He will find it as sure a precursor of his fate as Openshaw did before him.'

'And who is this Captain Calhoun?'

'The leader of the gang. I shall have the others, but he first.'

'How did you trace it, then?'

He took a large sheet of paper from his pocket, all covered with dates and names.

'I have spent the whole day,' said he, 'over Lloyd's registers and files of the old papers, following the future career of every vessel which touched at Pondicherry in January and February in '83. There were thirty-six ships of fair tonnage which were reported there during those months. Of these, one, the *Lone Star*, instantly attracted my attention, since, although it was reported as having cleared from London, the name is that which is given to one of the states of the Union.'

'Texas, I think.'

'I was not and am not sure which, but I knew that the ship must have an American origin.'

'What then?'

'I searched the Dundee records, and when I found that the barque *Lone Star* was there in January, '85, my suspicion became a certainty. I then inquired as to the vessels which lay at present in the port of London.'

'Yes?'

'The *Lone Star* had arrived here last week. I went down to the Albert Dock and found that she had been taken down the river by the early tide this morning, homeward bound to Savannah. I wired to Gravesend and learned that she had passed some time ago, and as the wind is easterly I have no doubt that she is now past the Goodwins and not very far from the Isle of Wight.'

'What will you do, then?'

'Oh, I have my hand upon him. He and the two mates, are as I learn, the only native-born Americans in the ship. The others are Finns and Germans. I know, also, that they were all three away from the ship last night. I had it from the stevedore who has been loading their cargo. By the time that their sailing-ship reaches Savannah the mail-boat will have carried this letter, and the cable will have informed the police of Savannah that these three gentlemen are badly wanted here upon a charge of murder.'

There is ever a flaw, however, in the best laid of human plans, and the murderers of John Openshaw were never to receive the orange pips which would show them that another, as cunning and as resolute as themselves, was upon their track. Very long and very severe were the equinoctial gales that year. We waited long for news of the *Lone Star* of Savannah, but none ever reached us. We did at last hear that somewhere far out in the Atlantic a shattered stern-post of a boat was seen swinging in the trough of a wave, with the letters 'L. S.' carved upon it, and that is all which we shall ever know of the fate of the *Lone Star*.